TAILS
TALES OF
TIME TRAVEL

WINNIE GARZA

Editing, formatting, and cover design by Katie Erickson, KatieEricksonEditing.com.

ISBN 979-8-9990674-1-8

This book is dedicated to my sons,
Landon and Shane Garza,
and to my grandchildren.

Thank you for making storytelling so much fun!

You have filled the pages in my heart,
where my own story is held,
with love, laughter, and adventure,
both real and imagined.

INTRODUCTION

What started out as pieces of a story written daily on my sons' brown paper lunch bags, about a hilarious talking dog, over the years, has become one of mystery and adventure.

You are invited to join the Heron family in one of their fantastical, whimsical adventures with Apples, the time-traveling Queen of Dog-World, and the friends they make along the way.

ACKNOWLEDGMENT

I really have to thank all the wonderful folks I know whose personalities, both serious and quirky, have been used in parts and pieces for characters in this book. Don't worry, though, your names have been changed to protect the innocent.

CONTENTS

CHAPTER ONE

AND SO IT BEGINS

"I knew she could find it!" Charlie's unmistakable whisper burst into the kitchen before he did.

"SHHhhh!"

"Yeah, we knew he was the one that did it! I bet it is still there, too! We are going to go get it now, and we will take the dog." Charlie continued whispering, grabbing the leash as he pulled on the cap he always wore sideways.

"Wait a minute, what? What are you talking about?" I asked from the kitchen.

"Dude! Charlie! You even *whisper* loud!" Christopher said as he glared at his younger brother, who rolled his brown eyes back at him.

To me, he began to explain, eyes wide, face flushed: "First, we saw Eddie take the missing money from the donation box at church. Remember that note that said, '*A fool and his money are soon parted. HAHA. April Fools*'? Then, it was the next day, and we saw him bury it in the dunes."

I couldn't believe what I was hearing. "April was two months ago! Why are you just now telling me you saw Eddie take the money? And you never told us you saw him bury it!"

"It was Apples, Mom. She showed us. She took us back in time?" Christopher told me, but with a question in his tone, hoping I believed this.

I had to admit there was something different, maybe even special, about our dog, Apples. She could talk, and she could read, but there was no way she could—could she?

"Don't tell them Ah can travel through time yet! Ahm do it, and don't tell that Christopher and Charlie went with meh that time. Ahm do it, too."

"Well, Apples, you just told them yourself. I am just trying to set the story up for the readers, and now, since you already have, I am sure they already think that you can travel through time!"

Anyway, as I was saying, our dog of course could talk, but believe it or not, having a dog that can talk does have its downside.

Apples can sometimes be rude, so when she says some things, people often think one of us humans has said it.

"Rude? When was Ah rude? Ahm never rude."

"Anytime you spout off with, 'Says who?' to people who are not even talking to you, and the way you interrupt conversations to put in your two cents—those are perfect examples."

"Well, you know that none of you are witty enough to come up with some of my better comebacks."

"Apples, I will thank you not to interrupt me while I tell this story."

"When, when are you gonna thank meh?"

"I will thank you right now: THANK YOU! Now, please go lie down."

"Well, Ah will thank you to tell the story properly then. Starting out by saying that Ah ahm some kind of a smarty mouth has hurt mah feelings, you know? Ah find it very interesting that no one thinks Ah ahm smarty mouth in Dog World."

"I, too, find that very interesting. I cannot imagine why they don't."

"There are two reasons. One, Ah ahm very funny. And two, Ah ahm the Queen of Dog World. Which, by the way, you forgot to mention!"

"Actually, Apples, I did not forget to mention it at all. You have interrupted me way too many times. I am just getting to that."

As you may have read, she claims to be the queen of a place she calls Dog World. We are not sure she always tells the truth, but we let her have her fantasies. We cannot prove she isn't a queen. I mean, she can talk, so....

"That's right, and Ah can read too! Ah ahm going to sit right here and make sure you tell the story correctly."

3

"That will not be necessary, believe me. I am going to tell it just the way it happened in real life. I mean here in this life. Oh, you know what I mean!"

"Believe meh, by now nobody knows what you mean. However, there is no cause for alarm. Ah ahm sure Ah can get you out of this mess. Here, you move over and Ah'll—"

"Never mind. I am sure I can straighten this out all by myself. Besides, you surely cannot type with those paws of yours!"

"Whose do you suggest Ah use? Ah type just fine with these paws! Of course, it ends up looking all doggish, but still Ah can type!"

"That is not the point. I am trying to tell these readers about you and about one of our family's adventures, but you keep interrupting me. Will you please stop long enough for me to properly introduce the readers to you and the rest of the family?"

"Ah suppose Ah can do that much, seeing that you're not going to let meh type, or anything else. Ah do hope though that you do not mind meh putting in mah two cents when it comes time to describe meh, for Ahm sure you do not have the ability to properly describe mah beauty. You owe meh that much at least!"

"Oh, for Pete's sake, Apples! Yes, I am quite sure that you alone should be the one to introduce yourself to our readers, but ... since you only type in doggish, I think it is better if I do it!"

Hello! I hope you will enjoy this time-traveling adventure that our family experienced, thanks to our time-traveling dog, Apples.

It all started when Apples began to live with us in the first place. Nothing too unusual, really. Our relationship started quite normally.

We are the Herons: my husband, Chet; myself, Betty; our two sons, Christopher and Charlie; and our girl, Emma.

Our boys wanted to have a puppy so badly when Emma was born, and before long she joined in on the hope of someday getting a puppy.

"Let's get a dog." "We need a puppy." "When will we get a dog?" was part of our daily dialogue for weeks—followed by promises of: "We will feed her, clean up after her, and walk her."

After much discussion and planning, we decided it was time to go ahead and get a pup.

"Mom, can we get a Dalmatian?" Christopher asked.

"No, Dalmatians are too expensive," I told him. "When we get a dog, it will be just an ordinary dog."

Charlie piped up with a question of his own: "If we found one for only $50, then, could we?"

I laughed as I answered, believing full well no Dalmatian would be priced that low: "HAHAHAA, well, if we did, yes!" But then I added, "I am pretty sure there will not be a Dalmatian puppy at the shelter, guys."

Now, who would have known that the very next day, when we all ran to the grocery store to pick up the needed items for the first cookout of the year on Memorial Day, those kids would run and check the bulletin board and find a paper plate that read, "Dalmatian Pup for sale $50.00"?

"HA, you should know it was mah doing! Ah did it. It was meh!" Apples giggled as she rolled around on her back. "It was a trick! Ah tricked you! WAA-waa-WAA-HAH! The best dog for any family would be meh, Ah always say!"

After the decision was made, we bought ourselves our puppy. We named her Apples because she was white with black spots of every shape and size all over her, just like an Appaloosa horse.

"Yah, it took meh about a year to forgive them for that name. They refused to call me by mah real name that is so much better. Mah real name is: 'OH, BEAUTIFULLEST QUEEN, HIGH ROYAL SUPREME ONE THAT IS LOVED AND CHERISHED BY ALL,' but Ah got used to Apples, so you can call me that for short—unless you are in Dog World. Then you have to address meh properly."

Not long after she settled in with us, we began hearing "the voice"—that's what we used to call it. The voice was a little higher-pitched than any of ours and sounded a lot more excited. Some words were a bit mispronounced, as you may have noticed. At first, we only heard the voice when she was given instruction or a new rule she didn't like.

"Well, what kind of kooks would not let the Queen of Dog World sit on the furniture, Ah want to know!"

Soon though, she was giving the orders. She hollered that Christopher was preparing her food wrong: not enough water and not mixed up enough!

"Put water in it; mix it up!"

Christopher thought Charlie was saying it, became angry, and told him to do it himself. Charlie denied saying anything, which resulted in them both rolling on the floor, legs and arms flying, punches thrown, a lot of yelling, and them both covered in wet puppy chow!

I think it was the minute she said, "What's a pup got to do to be fed properly around here?" that we finally realized that this crazy Dalmatian pup could talk. She was the one doing the extra blabbing, and we were going to have to get used to it. None of us found that a very easy task. The point is: Our dog could talk and is apparently the Queen of Dog World.

"Now Ah will take over at this point. You go ahead and do the typing; Ah will dictate. As you already know, Ah am the ruling Queen of Dog World. Ah have more power than most rulers, seeing that dog spelled backwards is God, if you know what Ah mean. Ah have certain powers that enable meh to do the impossible. Mah right eye is a beautiful blue eye. This wonderful eye winks and blinks when glorious things are about to happen or if a great idea pops into mah head. Mah other eye is equally as beautiful, but it is brown and circled with a black patch. You see, Ah ahm a patch pup, which means Ah have a big black patch on mah head that circles mah great brown eye. The magic in this eye is that in time of danger—or chores—this eye rolls around in its socket like a bowling ball. Not to bark up mah own tree or anything, but Ah really ahm the coolest, if you know what Ah mean."

All of this is true, and if that were all that was different about her, I would have to admit that she is indeed a very unique dog. There is, however, something else, something I did not know for quite a while after the children found out. You may have noticed that at the beginning of this story, Apples said for me not to tell you she could travel through time, and of course by saying it then, I probably do not need to tell you now, but just in case you were not too sure: It is true. She and many other dogs can really travel through time.

"What other dogs? Only us royal ones with a blue eye and a brown eye, which Ah have by the way, can time travel!"

"Wait a minute, you told me that you and your subjects got together in Dog World for sniff fests and pooping contests. Isn't that time travel?"

"Ah hardly would call that time travel, WAA-waa-WAA-HAA! Any dog can decide to go to Dog World and go. That is, if he or she was lucky enough to be left at home alone. Dogs simply watch out the window as the family car backs out of the driveway, run to the trash can, pick out the best garbage in it, and instantly they are in Dog World, which is located in the Canis Major constellation, known as the great dog. Ah also want people to know that mah poor subjects are not trying to make a big mess. They just want the coolest piece of trash! Ah might suggest to the readers to leave a great piece of garbage right at the top of the can, something like bones, balls, or old shoes. Old shoes are the best, by the way."

"I am sorry that I thought that meant all dogs could time travel."

"That is quite all right. Ah forgive you like any long-suffering friend would. It is not your fault you are not a dog, you know."

"Have I ever told you that I am fine with that, Apples?"

"Yes, you have, and it is a good thing too! You would be terrible at scaring squirrels, which, by the way, is the real reason we dogs inhabit the earth. Without us the world would *be crawling with the acorn-hoarding rodents! Mankind owes us a debt of gratitude, Ah would say!"*

"Apples, can we get back to the story please?"

"You have mah royal permission to do so."

"Oh, brother!"

This particular adventure started the summer after we first got Apples. She was just a bit over a year old, which made her seven in dog years. So, she was the same age as Emma, who was also seven; four years younger than Charlie, who was eleven; and five years younger than Christopher, who was the oldest at twelve.

June that year hit us hot and hard, and we could see it was certainly going to be a beach summer. We made sure the inner tubes and rafts had no leaks and that we all had fitting suits, sunglasses, beach towels, and sunscreen. And we dug out our big old picnic basket.

We fell into a routine of walking Apples after breakfast every morning. Life in West Michigan offers many trails through the dunes to choose from and great neighborhoods with bike trails and sidewalks to enjoy. At certain times in the year, when dogs are allowed, we could also choose to walk along the lakeshore. Our favorite place, though, was right through the local cemetery, in spite of the tales of it being haunted.

Yep, we were ready for the long, hot days ahead. At least we thought we were.

CHAPTER TWO

THE SNOW SNAKE

I am glad I did not know that the cemetery would be our main walking route that summer, because I may have decided not to go—and then we would have missed the adventure.

If I remember correctly, it was about day two or three of summer vacation before we decided to walk through Lake Forest Cemetery, one of our favorite places, because it is beautiful and we knew the shade there would be so nice.

"Wait, what about Eddie? Aren't you gonna tell them that you wouldn't allow meh and the boys to go get the missing money? Aren't you gonna say you were ah-scared? WAA-waa-WAA-HAA!"

Apples was on her back with paws on her stomach, her laugh more annoying than usual.

Such a drama queen—if queen of anything!

We did not know at the time about the gate, and certainly not about the path.

"Mom, look at this! A gate! We have never gone this way before." The sunlight shone on Charlie's face as he said this. His taller, thinner, dark-haired brother joined him as they piled the skateboards they had been riding along the path. "We're going in!" Christopher shouted as both boys left the tarred path and entered a sandy trail.

"Great," I muttered to myself. Emma and I sat on a nearby bench, while Apples sat, as if in deep thought, by one of the largest grave markers in the cemetery. As I glanced around, I liked how peaceful and pretty the cemetery was. Many of the graves had flowers that had recently been left by people who missed their loved ones very much. My heart went out to friends and family who had lost people close to them. I felt fortunate to have my loved ones so close and well. I quickly whispered a prayer of thanks.

The large statue we were sitting by was known as "the twin angels." They stood facing each other, one pointing to the north, the other toward the south, with their wings filling the air behind them. I never understood what this statue meant or what it stood for, and this particular day it seemed strange that the angel pointing north was pointing toward the path the boys took.

"It really is funny that we never noticed that path before," I said. Emma quickly agreed, her long-lashed blue eyes shining.

Apples added her two cents by saying that she had never seen it before, nor had she ever sniffed it, and she declared it to be old. "Yes, this is old, from another time, Ah think."

"Well, I surely do not know about that," I said. "Everywhere we go is as old as the earth and no older. I am just wondering where those boys have gone off to."

The path was somewhat overgrown, and it led to a grove of older trees. It was obvious that the boys had wandered into this forestlike area and equally obvious that I would have to go in and get them.

Apples, Emma, and I headed out of the main cemetery and soon could hear their voices in the distance. They were out heading through dunes where foxes, badgers, and even deer would live. Even though there was an occasional grave with markers that were leaning or had fallen down, this certainly was not the cemetery as we knew it. The only flowers left in remembrance were the ones God had put there. The forest floor was covered in beautiful Michigan wildflowers. I recognized the Pitcher's thistle, marsh marigolds, dwarf iris, and star flowers. I loved the smell of the damp earth. Right here in nature's air conditioner were the most gloriously fragrant smells of grasses and flowers, a rich herbal scent. I could understand wanting to be buried here. This was a very appealing place, this place of the dead. Suddenly, I shuddered. What on earth could I have been thinking things like that for? Then I felt sad, very sad.

"Christopher, Charlie!" Emma called.

"Hurry up! You're going to love this cool stuff we found!" one of the boys yelled. Emma practically tripped over her own feet as she ran to find them.

"Come on now, boys, we really need to get back if we are going to pack a picnic lunch before going to the beach." My own voice interrupted my thoughts. I did not want to stay here, but I honestly did not know why; this certainly was a pleasant enough place. I just could not shake that sad feeling.

It never would have occurred to me that we were not in our normal time. How could that be, anyway? I had not yet comprehended the concept of time travel. It was much easier for the kids.

"But Mom, this is sweet stuff! You've got to let Emma see it!" Christopher's voice was thin from the excitement.

"Wow!" Emma yelled. "This is the best-best-BEST!!!" As I rounded the curve in the path, I could see all their excited faces. "Can we please stay?" Emma's round blue eyes begged.

"Tomorrow, not now," I said. "Come along now, kids. We have to go."

The disappointment on all their faces added to the sadness I already felt. I should have let them stay a minute. What had come over me?

As we found our way back to the twin angels, Apples announced that her brown eye was rolling around like a bowling ball in her head.

"You know what it means if mah brown eye starts rolling, don't you?" she asked, then continued. "It means something is just not right! It means something is just plain wrong!"

"Of course something is wrong. We had to leave that awesome spot," Christopher said as he kicked a clump of dirt with all his might.

Apples said that was not it at all but that she would let us know as soon as she figured it all out.

It was very reassuring to me when we came out of the shaded cemetery into the sunlight. I had no understanding of what had just happened. I felt chilly and shivered.

"Yep," Apples said as she noticed the shiver, "something is just not right."

"Oh, be quiet," I demanded, then regretted it. The poor dog wasn't trying to be a bother.

Later on, while spending the afternoon at the beach, I realized that was the best way to get things off my mind. As I tanned, the kids were busy building sandcastles with their friends—and yes, Eddie was one of them—and seeing who could go out the farthest into the still-too-cold water. All this was followed by wave jumping.

As I watched the white-capped waves wash to the shore, it was as if they were washing that funny feeling I had in the forest away with them. I had to admit it was kind of nice that Apples was not allowed on the beach and I did not have to listen to her go on and on about her rolling brown eye!

We all agreed it had been a wonderful day. Of course, when we got home, we were reminded of the walk through the cemetery. Apples had been watching out our front window, waiting for us to come home. Our house is a bi-level, so its front window is up higher on the building, giving Apples a good view of anything that happens on our street. There she was barking at us as soon as she saw us round the curve at the top of the hill.

"She acts like we left her home alone for a week!" I exclaimed.

"Well, I gave her food and water," Christopher said. "Overreacting dog!"

"Plus, she can go to Dog World and get all the food and water she wants!" he added.

"We cannot believe everything that dog says, though, can we?" I asked.

To this Emma claimed, "I do! I believe her!"

"It's true," Charlie said. "We went to Dog World once with her. We told you, remember?"

Christopher interrupted then to say, "Mom told us not to ever mention that again. So why are you bringing that up now?"

"You brought it up, dummy!" Charlie shot back.

Emma, who just couldn't stay out of it, stuck her tongue out at Christopher, who responded by squirting her tongue with the spray sunscreen he was carrying. The wonderful day we had all agreed we'd had was coming to a pretty fast end!

Emma was the first to open the door because she obviously wanted to run in and rinse her tongue.

Apples immediately began to scold the boys. "Ah ought to slap you with mah tail—a good one that will send you sailing all the way to the shores of Wisconsin without a boat! In all mah years, which are many more than you know, Ah would've never thought that you boys would ever take anything that did not belong to you!"

Apples' brown eye was spinning as she spoke, and she was standing on her back legs shaking a paw in their faces!

"Apples, I can see you are upset, but I am still the mother around here, and if you think the kids have done something wrong, you need to tell me about it," I said. "Then I will decide whether or not they need a slap with your tail."

To the children I said, "Now, everybody calm down. Emma, go set the table. Christopher, throw the suits and towels into the washer. Charlie, put all the beach toys away, and I will start dinner. Dad will be home in about fifteen minutes. How do chili dogs and corn chips sound?"

"You mean, Ah can't swat them with mah tail? When can Ah swat them with mah tail?" Apples slumped to the floor.

"I am getting to that," I replied. "After we eat and are all calmed down, we will get to the bottom of this. Whatever has you so upset can at least wait that long. For now, you should just go lie down."

"Ah hate taking orders around here!" Apples said. "Ah still don't know what Ah did to deserve this."

We all love chili dogs, and for some reason, they were better that night than usual. Cleanup was quick, so we were ready to find out what had happened that had Apples all up in front legs (the canine version of "all up in arms," of course). Her brown eye was no longer spinning but still kind of swayed a bit. She was sitting up tall with a stick she had brought from Christopher's room. It was very smooth, about two feet long, and had a slightly curvy shape to it.

"This does not belong to you, and you need to return it," she said as she placed it on the floor in front of her.

Chet, who was new to the day's adventures, picked it up, turned it over, and took a long look at it. "I fail to see what all the excitement is about," he said. "It looks like a stick to me."

"You happen to be one hundred and fifty percent wrong about that," Apples said, annoyed. "This is no regular stick. They found it in the cemetery this morning and took it from a grave.

That is why mah eye rolled all the way home! Ah knew something was wrong. Now do you believe me?" she asked, looking from Chet to me, not even trying to hide her smirk.

Christopher and Charlie spoke in unison: "We didn't mean to be stealing anything!"

"There was a whole bunch of neat stuff that we just left there," Christopher said. "I just grabbed the stick when Mom said it was time to go."

Both boys had a "what's the big deal" look on their faces.

"Well, Ah can see that it is time for a little lesson." Apples sat up very straight and tall with a know-it-all look on her face as she spoke. "Number one," she said holding up a front paw, "this is not a stick. It is a snow snake, a toy used by Native American children to play a game. They would slide it across snow or ice, and whoever could slide theirs the farthest was the winner. Number two," up went her other front paw, "It belongs to the child it was buried with, which was not either of you, Ah might add! Number three, it has to be returned as soon as possible!"

We all laughed as she toppled over, as holding up three legs had been one too many!

"It is sacred," she added from the floor.

"Apples, are you implying that we were in an old Native American burial ground this morning?" I asked.

"Ah ahm not quite sure," she answered, then added, "not yet, anyway. The possibility is great. Hundreds of years ago, Native Americans, most likely the Odawa tribe, were the only people who lived here at all. On the other paw, it could be that there is only one, maybe two buried at that site."

"Why is it that you can tell us about the people that lived here hundreds of years ago, but you cannot tell us if this is an Odawa burial ground or not?" Chet leaned forward as he asked.

"That's easy, Dad," Charlie said. "Apples did not come into that part of the old cemetery, the part that has its own path. Right, Apples?"

"You are correct," Apples nodded.

"It was kind of a weird time travel, not a fully planned one," Apples said. "We went back in time, but you won't believe meh," she sighed.

"I think it is just the grave of one. We did not see any others," Christopher told us, then went on to describe the small area where the snow snake and other items lay. "There is a rectangle-shaped box made out of old logs on the ground, covered with old rotting leaves and a bunch of cool things scattered among the leaves."

"And a lot of cool bugs, too!" Charlie added.

"Ah plan on sniffing ninety miles an hour when we go back to return the snow snake," Apples declared. "Ah will know a lot more then, if you know what Ah mean!"

We all could tell Apples was ready for an adventure. I, on the other hand, felt unsure about going back to that strange place. I looked at Chet and said, "I just honestly do not think that I ever noticed that trail before this morning."

Apples interjected that she had not ever seen it before, either, but if she remembered correctly, and she was sure she did, I happened to be rubbing her ear at that time—which, according to her, is what makes time travel possible for humans.

"For once and for all, I will prove time travel is not possible, and I will use your own words to do it," I said. "Yes, I did, as a matter of fact, rub your ears in the cemetery, but I was not the one who noticed that trail. Christopher and Charlie saw it first. They were nowhere near your ears, so they were not rubbing them." I put all the mom authority I had into those words.

"True, they did not, but you were thinking of them at the time. You were thanking our heavenly Father for their health and safety, while Ah was wondering about how old this cemetery was," Apples explained. "That explains why the boys saw the trail and why you would not go any farther than you had."

Oh, now she could tell what I was thinking?

"I don't understand. What do you mean I would not go any farther than I had?" I asked.

"Simple," she replied. "You just do not believe, so this all scares you. You are afraid."

At first, I could not say anything. I remembered the feeling of sadness I felt there and how that feeling had been unsettling—with maybe a bit of fear mixed in, too.

Then I said, "I do not believe in time travel because it is not logically possible to do so."

"Well, that is where you make your mistake," Apples said. "There is absolutely no logic involved. What you need is the Queen of Dog World, and that happens to be a Dalmatian.

Dalmatians happen to be one of the oldest breeds of dogs. We have been around since early Egyptian times. We have seen it all, and we know it all. Now add the facts that Ah have a beautiful blue eye and an equally beautiful brown eye, which have both given meh amazing powers, and that mah ears, like all Dalmatian ears, are splendidly silky and blissful to rub. You just cannot lose! We can go anywhere! We can see anything! We can do whatever we want to do! You all are so lucky to know meh!"

At some point she had flipped over onto her back, with all four legs waving in the air!

It was Charlie who brought her back down to earth when he said, "Apples, we have rubbed your ears hundreds of times without flying off into another time. How come we could do that without traveling through time?"

"Wait a sec, we were rubbing her ears when we saw Eddie." Christopher bit his lower lip in thought.

"That is true," Apples said. "Ah have to admit Ah am kind of stumped by that one, but then, we were not really trying. Anyway, it works way better if we are summoned by someone else. Someone who needs us."

As she spoke, her blue eye started to wink and blink.

"You cannot possibly mean that—" I began to say when Christopher shouted, "Wow, we are in for one great summer!" and Charlie jumped to his feet, yelling, "I can't wait until tomorrow!"

Charlie gave his brother a fist bump. Emma joined in with an exuberant, "Yes!" as she executed a perfect fist pump.

I laughed as I looked at Chet, who had a very amused look on his face. "They really do believe all this stuff, don't they?" he asked. Then he answered his own question by stating, "Yes, they sure do, and one thing is for sure, that entertainment should be free for the next few years with this crazy dog around. Time travel has not been disproved, you know. Maybe we can rub her ears, go back to the theme park in Florida we went to last year, and relive it all!"

"All right!" the kids hollered.

I was about to object when Apples shouted, "No way! Who would want to go there? They make that canine guy seem so goofy, like a big nut or something! Ah could not do it; Ah won't do it. It would not be right to do!"

After a good laugh, we realized it was time for bed, and everyone, after their usual protests, settled down. Everyone, that was, except for Apples. When I went through the house turning off lights, she was stationed at the window, her brown eye rolling just slightly.

CHAPTER THREE

MOON-DEER

The first voice I heard the next morning was, of course, Apples'. She was informing the kids that it was time to go return "what was so wrongfully taken." I was barely able to get dressed fast enough to stop them at the door.

"Hold on one minute," I said. "Nobody goes anywhere until the breakfast is eaten and the chores are done. You all know what to do, and if you get busy, we can go in about half an hour or so."

Charlie protested. "Oh, Mom, can't we just forget the chores this one time?"

When the other two began their protests, Apples interrupted them to say, "Ah told you all to do your work first, now, didn't Ah? Why you all will not learn to listen to meh I just do not know. Ah just cannot figure that one out!" Then she asked me if I wanted her to slap them with her tail!

The kids started arguing with her, agreeing that she had *not* told them to do their chores. I already knew she hadn't because I heard every word she said.

"It doesn't matter what she did or did not say," I said firmly, turning to Apples and looking her straight in the eye. "The last time I checked I was still the mother of this family, and in this house, mothers have more power than queens!"

"Ah do not know why Ah put up with this!" she sighed and thumped to the floor to wait for the rest of us.

"Simple! You love to eat," I said, reaching down and patting her head. I caught myself avoiding touching her ears. *You're just being silly*, I thought to myself. *Nothing will happen.* Nevertheless, I did not touch them. I could tell by the goofy look on her face that she knew what I was thinking.

"Yah, Ah can and Ah will thank you to not use the word 'goofy' when describing meh!"

Right after morning chores were finished, we set out on our walk to the cemetery to return what was apparently a Native American artifact.

"Are you sure we have to return this?" Christopher wondered. "Can't we just keep it? I mean, what is the worst thing that can happen to us if we do not return it?"

"I am not sure anything would happen," I explained as we walked, "but I do feel it would be wrong to keep it, because the Native Americans believed that when they died, they went on into another life. I think they referred to it as their 'final journey.' They buried items they felt would be useful to them as they journeyed into the afterlife."

Charlie commented that he did not realize I knew anything about Native Americans. I was embarrassed to admit that I knew very little, even though I knew we did have some Native American blood in us.

"I wish we could learn more about them," Christopher replied.

Emma added that we must not have very much Native American blood left in us since we don't know very much about them.

"If you want to know anything about them, you could just ask meh!" Apples said excitedly.

"Yes, well, I have been meaning to talk to you about that," I said. "I want you all to understand that we are simply returning the snow snake today. If we want to learn more about our Native heritage, we will go and visit the library." I was trying to sound as firm as I possibly could.

We were now at the entrance of the cemetery. The shade from the tall oaks cooled our faces, and we could already tell it was going to be a hot day. Shade and light tickled across our faces in some kind of tag game, moving with the leaves rustling in the soft breeze above.

We took the familiar road that led to the twin angels, but none of us was in too much of a hurry. We would return the snow snake together, and I was determined not to be overwhelmed with sadness. I hoped my curiosity would overcome that. Maybe the kids had discovered something that was long forgotten or things we didn't even know had existed.

We all became a bit more excited as we approached the twin angels. Our excitement quickly turned into bewilderment when none of us could find the gate or the path that had been there yesterday. It was neither to the right nor to the left of the angel statue that had seemed to point the way.

"Anyone up for some ear rubbing?" Apples asked.

"Come on, Mom, can we?" Christopher asked. "It is the only way we can return the snow snake." He looked so hopeful. So many thoughts went through my mind. Foremost was the thought that when this didn't work, it may just put an end to the silly idea of a time-traveling dog, but if it did work—well, there was no way this would work, right?

"Remember, you did it by accident yesterday, and nothing bad happened," Charlie was quick to add.

"Oh, for heaven's sake, the path has to be here somewhere," I said, frantically trying to part the brush in the overgrown area where the path had been.

"I can't even get through this, and I am the littlest one!" Emma exclaimed.

"Mom, we've done it before."

"It was not scary or dangerous."

"And it was not our imagination."

"It really is Apples; she is the Queen of Dog World, and—"

I couldn't tell who was saying what because they were all talking at once. To put an end to this nonsense, I bent down, took the dog's ears in my hands, and rubbed them.

It was that quick and easy, nothing more, nothing less. The path appeared just like it had yesterday, and one by one I followed my kids into the woods and over the dune. I realized that this was not yesterday, but many yesterdays ago. How many? I did not know. We walked through the older part of this cemetery, the headstones broken, weathered, and forgotten. Charlie was leading the way, telling us, "It's this way," or, "Turn here," as the old graves grew fewer in number. I felt the sadness return as we approached an archway made by the tall trees and entered into a long-ago forgotten glade deep into the forest. Just as they had said, there laid a rectangle made of logs, the grave, just as they had described it: with those leaves and all the cool items. Thankfully, there were no remains of a body. Of course, this just added to the mystery.

"Mom, where is he or she, you know, the person who was supposed to be here?" Emma asked.

"He is hiding behind a tree waiting to come out and grab you!" Christopher said spookily, shaking his hands in her face. "BOOOoooOOOO!"

As Christopher bent over to replace the snow snake, I answered her question the best I could.

"I don't know, but maybe he was moved for some reason." I sat on the edge of one of the logs, and immediately, my sadness changed to deep grief. As tears began to fill my eyes, I knew that I was not the only one who felt this sorrow.

Right before us stood a Native American woman, weeping as if her heart was breaking. I felt like mine was going to as well if I did not leave that place.

"Mom, I feel so sad." Emma, who had noticed my tears, was also beginning to cry.

"I just feel lost," Christopher said.

"Me too," added Charlie.

The woman seemed to be unaware of us. I was not liking the situation and could not figure out what any of it meant. Yesterday, I did not believe any of this could even be possible.

Now we were right in the middle of something really weird, and I still was trying to deny the possibility that time travel could be true. I just thought we needed to get out of there. As I got up to go, I took Emma and Charlie by the hand, and Christopher automatically followed my lead.

Apples, of course, sat stubbornly in front of us, saying, "Well, Ah cannot believe what Ah ahm seeing. Ah ahm ashamed of all of you. Don't be such scaredy-cats!"

She then marched over to the woman and began to speak to her in a language we did not understand. The woman, however, did understand and answered Apples in the same language that Apples had used. She hugged Apples, but she still seemed unaware of us until I saw Apples point at us with her front paw. Her eyes met mine then, and our eyes stayed fastened on one another for a moment before she spoke to me.

"You are a mother, like me," she said as Apples interpreted for us. "Help me find my son."

I suddenly understood the sadness and grief I felt there. She had lost her boy and would grieve until he was found. I do not believe anything could be worse than losing a child. I felt a strong bond with this woman as one mother to another often does, yet it seemed to be stronger than that.

She then bent down and retrieved the snow snake from the grave. She handed it to Christopher and said, "You are a boy much like my son."

Her eyes said so much more than her words. They were pleading with us to help her do what the passing of time had not done: to heal her heart and spirit. To accomplish this, we would have to find her son.

Apples continued to interpret for us and explained that her boy went missing three hundred years ago. His mother and family knew he was dead, but his spirit had not yet crossed over the path of souls.

I think I made some sort of promise to help. I knew I wanted to help, and I could tell by looking at the kids' faces that they would do all they possibly could to help, too.

This time it was Apples who decided we should leave. As we left, we could hear the mother sing in her native tongue. The song, I was sure, was a prayer. In my own spirit I felt I understood every word. As we left the path, we were not surprised that, once again, it disappeared.

"Wow, I don't even know what the path of souls is," was all I could mutter.

Charlie said, "See, Mom, we told you, didn't we?"

Christopher added, "Now you believe us, right?"

Emma, almost in a whisper, said, "Now you don't think they made this all up, do you?"

Three days into the summer vacation of 1987, we knew that what just happened was very special. I knew I would most likely never understand this, but I knew we had to follow our hearts.

We had been asked for help from another time, and somehow, someway, we were going to do just that!

As I bent down to hug Apples, she whispered in my ear that the boy we would look for belonged to the Odawa tribe, and his name was Wind-Traveler or Wanderer.

"There is a saint named St. Christopher who is the patron saint of travelers," I whispered back. I quickly saw the connection the Odawa woman had felt toward Christopher and wanted to help her all the more.

I was still thinking about our morning as I sat at the beach with an open book in my lap. It was as if I could see what this same shoreline must have looked like three or four hundred years ago. The kids were in the water on inner tubes, and I couldn't help but picture canoes that once ran through the same water. I thought about wigwams that sat off into the dunes and the people who had called this land home.

Suddenly, I was frustrated with myself for not knowing more about my heritage. I should know more about it, and I needed to know more about it. How could I help the Odawa mother when I knew so little? These thoughts and feelings followed me the rest of the day. I can't deny I thought that maybe I had lost my mind! I wondered if Chet would think we were all nuts and decide to sell Apples to the circus!

It didn't help that, as Chet was paying at the door for the two large pepperoni pizzas we ordered for dinner, Apples yelled from just out of view, "Ah will thank you to put one of those pizzas into the dog dish, sir!"

"Next time Ah ahm gonna say, 'You know what to do with the pizza, and Ah will thank you to do so!' WAA-waa-WAA-HAH!"

"Apples, for heaven's sake! I am trying to keep you from being sold to a circus! Just behave! Now don't start interrupting again so I can continue this story." I patted her head, and she sighed as she dropped to the ground, as if she was disgruntled with the whole world.

With mouths full and a couple of spilled pops, all three of the kids excitedly related the day to their dad. I just sat there watching Chet's face, not saying a word, just barely able to keep up with who was saying what.

"Odawa mother."

"Lost boy."

"Secret path."

"Empty grave."

With a lot of "snow snake" thrown in.

Chet's reaction took me by surprise: "I knew it! I knew it! Boy oh boy, I tell you anything is possible!" He ended his sentence with a loud clap.

"Are you kidding?" I asked, stunned. "You don't think we are all crazy?"

"Why would I be kidding?" he asked. "I have believed that time travel was possible since I was Christopher's age. I knew that someday something like this would happen. Don't you realize that God created time for the events of mankind? There has to be an outside of time!"

"I guess if you believe that, it explains how we got the Queen of Dog World for a dog, then," I said, smiling at Apples.

"It also explains why you all were asked to help, in case you did not know," Apples added.

"Apples, the day we picked you up at that strange little house and you were sitting next to a bucket with a note that said,

'Leave check, take pup,' were you? Did you?" Chet asked with squinted eyes and wrinkled forehead.

"Ah told you it was meh! *WAA-waa-WAA-HAH!*" Apples laughed.

"I just hope the neighbors don't end up thinking we are all crazy, if they don't already," I sighed.

"Ah have very little time to concern mahself with what the neighbors are thinking," Apples said, "and Ah really don't care." She was sitting up tall, and we knew she was taking the floor. "As you know, Ah spoke to Moon-Deer in her own tongue. Moon-Deer, the Odawa mother's name, told me that her son, Wanderer, had disappeared on one of the yearly travels that the Odawa take before winter. Many years they looked for him, but never found him, not in body and not in spirit. As you know, the Odawa people buried their dead with the things they thought they would need on their journey to the next life. Wanderer never came to collect the things he would need. His mother has come and asked us for help, hoping we can help him find his way. She has waited nearly three hundred years for his spirit to come to her, and she sings songs of prayer to the Great Spirit for guidance as she waits."

Apples said all that without sounding too much like a know-it-all. I was very impressed.

"We might be the answer to her prayer," Christopher said softly.

Emma asked the question I think we all wanted to ask: "Is Moon-Deer dead or alive?"

Apples answered, "Moon-Deer is only dead the way we look at death. Her spirit, like ours, will live on in the spirit world, which, as far as Ah ahm concerned, is more real than this earthly one. She knows her son should be with her in spirit and believes he somehow lost his way."

"There are still so many unanswered questions," Chet said, deep in thought.

"Yah, Ah agree, but we will find out more as we continue," Apples said. "You might find this hard to believe, but even Ah do not know everything."

"That, oh mighty queen, is what I have been telling you for a whole year now," I said, laughing. At this point, she just looked at me, her head cocked over to one side with the questioning look dogs use when they just don't know what you mean.

Charlie asked, "Do you think we should go back further in time? Like before Wanderer disappeared?"

"That is exactly what I was thinking, Charlie," Chet said. "If we go back too far, though, it could do more harm than good, and we don't want that to happen. We will have to find him in his spirit and guide him to his mother's spirit. If we find him living, it could change too much of history."

"Yah, she chose to wait at his grave, and we cannot do a thing to change that," Apples informed us.

"Good! Then we are looking for a ghost, aren't we?" Christopher asked excitedly.

I looked at all their faces and said, "Yes, we are, and we may have already met one. I hope we can turn sorrow into joy for Moon-Deer."

Apples wasted no time in pointing out that when people travel through time, they are not seeing ghosts—they are seeing living people in whatever time they have traveled to.

As I looked at Chet's handsome face, I wondered where Wanderer's father was. Had he tried to talk Moon-Deer out of staying behind? Those and other unanswered questions swirled through our heads as night fell in around us.

CHAPTER FOUR

THE ODAWA

CHILLICOTHE

The thunderstorm the weatherman had promised arrived in full rolling action by morning.

In Michigan, we learn to go with whatever the weather dictates. If it is hot and sunny, go to the beach. If it is raining, catch up on laundry! Of course, I am talking about summertime, as in winter things are a bit different. Anyway, it may sound odd, but it usually rains at least once a week or thereabouts, so that is plenty of time to catch up on laundry or some deeper cleaning. The kids, however, hated the boring rain. They hated the answer I always gave them when they complained about it more, though: "Go clean your room if you are so bored." Suddenly, they were not so bored as they scrambled to go play Pac-Man or Super Mario Brothers.

"Are you going to continue boring the readers with your housekeeping tips, or do Ah have to take over telling the story now?"

"You are right, Apples, I am sure they would rather me get on with the story. Now, where was I? Oh yes."

Rain or no rain, Apples still had to go out to do her dog business and get a good walk in for exercise.

"Ah have to keep the squirrels under control, you know," she said.

So, after throwing a load of laundry in the wash and grabbing an umbrella, I got her leash and went for what I thought would be a quick walk. Before I realized it, we were headed straight for the cemetery. The twin angels stood silently in the rain as I rubbed Apples' ears. The path appeared, and we literally ran to the place of Wanderer's empty grave. Moon-Deer was there as she had been the day before, standing, not seeming to mind the rain. I looked at her for a few moments. What was I looking for? What was it that I wanted to know?

Her black hair was in braids down to her waist and wet from the rain. Although she was dressed simply, she possessed a strength and a beauty that could not be denied. She looked at me then and spoke one word: "Odawa." She knew I would know that word, and she knew, even though I had not, that this is what I came to find out. I looked more closely at her face, very much like the face of my own grandmother, very much like my own face. Could she be my ancestral grandmother?

"Odawa," she spoke again, and this time her hands went from her heart toward me with palms up.

Apples had sat silently during this short meeting and understood that this was something I had to find out for myself. Suddenly, I knew that I and my family belonged to the Odawa. We were her own people, and the boy we were looking for was my ancestral uncle!

"That is not why Ah sat silent! Ah just wanted to speed things up! Ah was getting rained on, and it was ruining mah hairdo!"

"Oh, nonsense, Apples! You don't even have a hairdo!"

Anyway, I decided to let the kids figure this all out in their own way. They loved figuring out things on their own. I smiled, knowing this would be so much fun for them.

The rain continued for two more days, and we put them to use by going to the library and getting out all the books we could on Native Americans, mostly what we could find on the Odawa tribe. It wasn't hard to figure out why the county we lived in was called Ottawa County, but it sure made what was becoming a crazy summer seem more real. We learned all we could from the books, but what we all really wanted to do was to go back in time and see it for ourselves.

"Man, I wish we could go back and see how they really lived before Wanderer was dead, but we can't because it would mess up history," Christopher said.

Apples said, "We will go back during the years his family searched for him and experience how they lived without causing any problems—that's mah plan!" I could see the dog was just as excited as the kids were.

"We just need to remember the 'take nothing but memories and leave nothing but footprints' rule," I said, then added, "whenever we do try again." I was still in disbelief about it all.

"Let's try to go back before there was a grave for him," Charlie said, his brown eyes filled with excitement and his grin nearly wrapped around his head!

"I am going to try and find a girl to be friends with when we go next time," Emma said, causing the boys to groan.

At least it seemed we had a plan now. The rain had not dampened our determination to keep our promise to try to find what happened to Wanderer and send him on the journey to find his people. We thought the next day would be a perfect day to try, but before that next day came, we all woke up in the middle of the night.

"Help me! Help!"

Was that Christopher? We all hurried to his room to find him thrashing in bed. He was having a nightmare and woke up when I said his name. "I dreamed I was drowning, and no one was there to help me."

"We are here now, and you are OK," I said, hugging him. As I went back to bed, I was grateful knowing that my kids were all safe and sound in their own beds.

That next day did become "today" bright and early. Toast and cereal disappeared as quickly as it was served up, dishes found their way into the dishwasher, and chores almost seemed to be doing themselves. Faces were washed, teeth were brushed, and the dog was put on a leash when—suddenly their bubbling excitement turned into quiet expectation.

"Are you sure you all want to do this?" I asked. They all nodded.

"Wanderer's journey is way too important for us not to go," Christopher said.

"And important to his mother, too," I added.

"It matters to the whole tribe," we all said in unison.

As we opened the door to head out on a journey of our own, Chet pulled into the driveway. "Come on, tribe," he said coincidentally, "I took the day off work for this."

The tall trees, green grass, purple lilacs, and blue skies filled with happy little clouds all seemed to be in on our secret. We were time travelers, and we had a job to do.

"Go ahead, rub her ears, Chet," I said.

"I would, but I am not sure what to think about, and actually now it feels silly," he replied.

I had to laugh at his confused expression—he was the one who had believed in time travel since he was a boy!

"Maybe we should think of Wanderer when he was playing with the snow snake," Emma said.

"No, that would be too far back. Remember, we are not supposed to see him in the flesh," Chet reminded her.

"Oh yeah, just his ghost," Emma sighed.

"I think we should concentrate on how we think his family felt when they could not find him," Christopher suggested.

"That is a good idea," I agreed. "I know the first day we came out here, I was thinking about how sad it would be to lose someone you loved and how thankful I am for all of you."

Apples was in total bliss as the ear rubbing began. We all concentrated on the boy's family, and—nothing happened.

"Maybe you rubbed them the wrong way!" Emma said.

"No way! How can you rub a dog's ear wrong?" asked Charlie.

Lord, maybe we are all out of our minds, I thought, but did not say.

"Wait a minute! It's starting to come back to meh now!" Apples put her head on the ground, with her two front paws over her eyes, while her tail swished slowly back and forth across the grass. "Umm, ahh, woo, heh, heh, oh yah, yah ohhh!"

Chet rolled his eyes as the boys shifted their weight from side to side, and Emma happily collected up a handful of wildflowers.

"Oh, come on!" I said.

Just then she hollered with her head still down, "WAH HOO!! Ah got it, Ah got it! There is a trick to group travel. There are too many of you trying to travel at one time right now, but since you are not asking meh what the secret is, Ah do not have to tell you," she said as she slipped one paw away from her blue eye to see our reaction.

"There is only one more of us than last time," I pointed out.

"Well, that is one more too many, and now Ahm not telling you!"

"You crazy dog, you want to tell us as badly as we want to know!" Chet said as we all laughed.

"I am kind of glad it didn't work the first time," Emma said. "I forgot to think about making friends with the Odawa girls."

"Are you sure you have it figured out now?" I asked.

"Maybe you do not want to go after all! Ahm trying to tell you about group travel, and you are not the least bit interested," Apples said. "Ah have a hard time believing that anything Ah do is not extremely interesting, if you know what Ah mean. Ah cannot help it if Ah ahm still trying to figure out mah amazing powers. Ah ahm only one year old in human days. It takes meh awhile every time Ah zip to another time to relearn how cool Ah ahm, you know? Now, what you do not know is: *Two* of you have to rub mah ears and think about the same thing, and everyone else has to hold hands with the people that rub! Hold tight, and off we will go!"

I noticed her blue eye winking as Christopher and Charlie each had an ear.

"No thinking about girls," Charlie said.

"Time to get serious," Chet said, grasping Charlie's hand. I had Christopher's and Emma's.

Three short seconds later the gate and old path appeared. We did not walk far before we were right in the center of the Odawa camp. We took in the sights of wigwams set up in a circle formation and people busy with their everyday tasks, baskets of freshly caught fish and just-picked berries ready to dry in the sun. The children were running and laughing, chasing one another where, just a couple of days ago (for us, anyway), was an old broken-down and forgotten graveyard.

"This makes me sad to think that right here, where they had full lives, we only know as a place for graves," Charlie said.

"Like it represents the death of their nation," Christopher added with frustration in his voice.

"I feel like we are intruding and do not belong," I said.

"Well, remember, we were summoned here to help, so we are not intruding!" Chet wanted to reassure us.

Emma took off running in the direction of a group of girls her age, yelling over her shoulder that she had found friends. I thought about stopping her, but it was obvious that the Odawa people had no idea we were there.

Emma returned shortly, disappointed that they did not see her.

"We are not here today so that they can see you, but so that we see them," Apples said. "After all, that is why we came back this far—to learn more about their ways. There is more for you to learn, and if Ah were you—which, by the way, Ah ahm glad Ahm not—Ah suggest you do so quickly, so start paying attention to what is going on." Apples' blue eye was beginning to wink and blink. Motioning with her paw toward the village, she explained it was called a *chillicothe,* and a group of wigwams was called a *canada.*

Now, I would have to make a lot of this up if I tried to remember everything we said or how each one of us felt as individuals, so I will try and hit the highlights. I know we sat on the grass in the shade, and I realize that sometimes one or two of us moved around to get a closer look, but let me tell you we watched—in total fascination and awe.

It was amazing that their homes and canoes were all provided from the pine, birch, beech, and oak trees from the wooded dunes surrounding them. Plants and wildlife provided them with food and clothes.

Their wigwams were made from young trees or small branches. We watched the young men, with tattooed torsos and pierced noses, bend them into an arch-shaped frame and put the ends into the holes others had dug. The half-barrel shape took a more recognizable form when smiling and talkative women tied the frame together for support with roots from pine trees they had gathered at an earlier time.

One man called Running Bear must have said something funny as long strips of birch bark were laid over the frame. Laughter followed and seemed to encourage more joking and fun. I wondered if the couple who were securing the bark with pine sap would move into the wigwam, as they seemed to be flirting and in love. More laughing, teasing, and flirting followed as they tied additional roots over it all until the wigwam was completely covered. I couldn't help but go and take a closer look at what, I was sure, would soon be the home of this young couple. The finishing touch seemed to be the soft-needled pine boughs that were placed on the dirt floors for softening them. I loved the wonderful smell of fresh pine that filled the dwelling.

Nearby, several young men were using the same materials and methods to build a canoe. They used white cedar to build a frame, covered it with birch bark, sewed it together using pine roots as thread, and finally sealed the seams with pine sap.

This especially interested Christopher and Charlie. I could see ideas forming in their heads as they agreed with each other that they would be making some pretty cool forts and maybe even a canoe someday using these methods.

Men and women returned from fishing and were soon adding some of their fish to the others drying in the sun, while some would be that night's meal. Several women with babies in cradleboards on their backs and running children nearby came with baskets of berries to do the same. We watched as a few tended gardens, and I knew that some of the corn, squash, and beans would also be dried and stored for the winter. They all had jobs to do and seemed very content to do them. They were a happy and contented people. There was much talking and laughing as they worked, and I was proud to be among them.

The hunters were the last to return for the day. They were greeted with gladness and their contributions taken care of. Many rabbits and squirrels and two deer were presented to the group, a very good day for the tribe. Hunters and gatherers alike would give thanks to the Great Spirit and celebrate these gifts.

After the evening meal of fish and some type of fried bread was finished, the fire in the center of the camp was built up, signifying that the evening would soon come to a close. Slowly, the people gathered around, sitting or squatting with children kept nearby.

Oh, how we all wished we could understand the stories that were shared around that fire! Apples couldn't interpret for us because she was off with her dog friends—or should I say subjects? We laughed when the Odawa people laughed, and when their faces showed fear, we were scared, too. One storyteller spoke softly, and we watched as tears were shed on their beautiful brown faces—we were actually moved to tears along with them. Our spirits grasped onto some concepts that our heads weren't able to understand.

A very important man stood as songs of thanks were then offered to the Great Spirit for the good things this day had provided. With arms outstretched, his deep voice filled the air with his native language. The star-filled sky above seemed to settle in to watch and to listen as the tall feathers on his headdress danced for them. The animal skins he wore moved with him, and the rattling of the bear claws around his neck kept time. We had learned at the library that a man like this was the medicine man, a spiritual leader for these people. He was the keeper of myths, legends, traditions, and tribal wisdom. It was believed that he also had the supernatural ability to heal and to protect his tribe from evil. Many joined him in song and prayer. I noticed several of the children had fallen asleep as the rhythm of the drums calmed us all.

We all recognized Moon-Deer when she joined the man in dance. Her face was kissed with moonlight as she looked to the night sky, and her long, braided hair shone where the moon softly touched it, making it appear blue. Moon-Deer no longer dressed in a simple deerskin, but in a ceremonial dress adorned in shells and dyed porcupine quills. As she moved, dyed grasses in her hair and the quills on her dress swayed in the firelight.

The mesmerized looks on the faces of my kids matched my feelings. We were all definitely drawn into the scene.

As the themes of the songs went from sorrow to hope, we felt that it was time for us to go, so, feeling like we learned a bit but accomplished very little, we returned to our own time. We stood in bright daylight where the path had been. No time had passed in our world, and it was still early in the day.

"They were praying to the Great Spirit for help in finding Wanderer, weren't they?" Christopher asked.

"I am sure of that," Chet replied. "What I am not sure of is how we fit into all of this. How do we help an Odawa boy that has been lost about three hundred years journey into the next life?"

"I don't know, but I do know it is hot enough for an ice cream cone, and I know a place we can get one," Emma said. She usually suggested ice cream when she didn't know what else to do. Her idea was a hit with the rest of us, so off we went to pick out our favorites: Superman for Christopher, bubblegum for Charlie, mint chocolate chip for me, chocolate almond for Chet, and garbage can for Emma. We told her it was just all the other leftover flavors scraped into one container; she never believed it.

"Ah noticed that you did not mention that Ah received no ice cream whatsoever."

"Apples, we agreed that I would tell the story, remember?"

"OK, OK, Ah just wanted to point out to mah fans how you treat the Queen of Dog World, you know."

"Your fans most likely know that dogs are not allowed into ice cream shops, so if you will go lie down or just go to Dog World for a minute, I will continue...."

"Well! Ah ahm sure that they also realize that queens are allowed in stupid old ice cream shops, and Ah bet the readers are as outraged about this as Ah ahm!" She was holding both of her front paws to her chest, looking as perplexed as she possibly could.

"They are going to be more outraged if they are not able to find out what happened to Moon-Deer and Wanderer because of your interruptions. Now, be still."

CHAPTER FIVE

EDDIE

We did our best to keep up with our usual summer activities over the next few weeks. Swimming and lifesaving lessons at the Y, dinners at the beach, music lessons, ball games, and cookouts with our good friends the Muldunes took much of the time we might have spent trying to help Wanderer and his family. In a way, I was glad for that. I wanted to keep our lives as normal as we possibly could with a time-traveling dog in the house. So, normal became a secret goal of mine, we hadn't been summoned for a few days as Apples pointed out—and honestly, none of us had a clue what we could do to help.

We were sure that we must be able to do something or Moon-Deer would have never reached across time to ask us. We continued to study up on the Odawa way of life. We visited several libraries and museums. We did not find too much on what their religious beliefs were, but we learned of the respect all things were given by the Odawa: Each living creature and each item used possessed a spirit. The spirit of man needs the spirit of a thing, whether a moccasin, a tool, or a bowl. All things were treated as if they had life.

Life in all forms was treated with great respect. All things had a purpose or use, and nothing was wasted. I think we would not have to be so concerned with our environment in modern times if we treated the earth the same way. The Native Americans did not take what they could not use, and they did not have problems with landfills or pollution. Our family realized that there was a lot we could do about these problems and decided to do our part. We started recycling everything we could and put having a thankful heart for the things we had into practice. Gratefulness, we learned, deepens your respect for all you have.

We were well into the second week of July, and Vacation Bible School started bright and early on Monday morning. Our family was on snack detail that day. I was just setting up the snack table when Eddie jumped to his feet, his black curls bouncing, and declared, "Jesus! What do you want to know about Jesus?" With one finger held up, he said, "One, He was born on Christmas," and when the second finger joined the first, he added, "two, He died on Good Friday," and holding up a third finger, "three, He rose on Easter!"

What Eddie had said was true, and we all laughed. Eddie was an orphan who lived with Beulah, his grandmother. We all liked him in spite of his mischievous ways, but what he just said reminded Christopher and Charlie about seeing him take the donation money from the church and then take it to the dunes. No one wanted to get Eddie in trouble, so when our eyes met across the room, we had agreed in silence to find a better, more loving way to deal with him.

Christopher and Charlie wanted to go up to the dune on the lakeside instead of through the cemetery to see what else we might see and possibly to find the missing money. It was a good idea, so after chicken salad sandwiches, potato chips, grapes, peanut butter cookies, and cold pop were packed and sunscreen slathered on, we were ready to go.

"Well, Ah knew they wanted to spy on Eddie again! Ah was right. Right? WAA-waa-WAA-HAA!"

"You're getting ahead of the story again, Apples. Just sit tight a minute."

"Ah personally love the idea of climbing up the front of the dune," Apples, who insisted that we tie a bag of her dry food to her collar, said. Then she added, "Ah have been meaning to get up this way mah whole life to check out the squirrel situation."

"You picked out a perfect day for this hike." Chet, who had a short workday, surprised us as we headed toward the dune.

The sky was baby blue with just a touch of the gentlest clouds floating about, bright white against the blue. A very slow, steady breeze greeted us from off the lake. Although the breeze was warm, it promised to keep us comfortable.

I always loved the contrast between water and sand at the beach. With each wave of water, I watched as the patterns in the sand were playfully rearranged.

"This would be a perfect day for the beach, too," Emma said, looking out over the lake from the dune.

"Yes, it would," I said. "Now, aren't you glad I had you put your suit on under your clothes? We will all be ready for a quick dip."

"I hope we packed enough food for a day at the beach, too," Charlie said as he rubbed his slightly rounded tummy.

Chet was quick to say, "There is no need for the extra food. I plan on having Apples return us all to about five minutes before we originally eat our lunch, and that way we can eat the same lunch twice."

"EWWWW, Dad, that is gross, like eating puke!" Emma's face was totally distorted when she responded to what Chet had said.

"And what is wrong with that, may Ah ask?" Apples asked, confused.

Christopher explained that while some dogs may do that, humans do not.

"Well, Ah hope you know it is for a very good reason," Apples was quick to say. "However, Ah will never tell you or any other hind-legged walkers what that reason might be."

"That is good—none of us wants to know," I said as I adjusted the bag of sandwiches I was carrying from one shoulder to the other.

Chet ended the discussion by admitting he was only kidding; we would have plenty of snacks at the beach, and dinner would be at the Muldunes' house later. No one needed to be worried about food. We would be taken care of.

We chose the top of the dune to eat lunch because the view was so beautiful. The sun was getting higher and hotter, so we headed up into the trough dunes where some trees stood for a bit of shade. We sat enjoying our lunch and admiring how the blue water met the blue sky. An occasional white-capped wave and the red lighthouse down the shore were the only breaks in all that blue. Even the clouds were gone now; they had danced away with the breeze.

Of course, there was still the golden sand gleaming from the shoreline all the way up to where we were sitting.

The beach area shoreline, known as the foredunes, is actually quite a harsh environment. With the exception of scattered beach grass waving in the breeze, nothing grows there. Sand temperatures can reach up past two hundred degrees Fahrenheit when the sun beats down all day. Then in the darkness of night the temperatures drop dramatically, making it impossible for plant life to develop. No plant life, no animals, and, in fact, very few insects survive in what is almost a little desert in a beautiful oasis.

As we cleaned up after lunch, Christopher said he thought we needed to plan exactly when and where we would like to be when we leave so that we can be of the most help.

"You know, that is true," Chet said. "I enjoy learning about the ways of this people as much as the rest of you, but we have been asked for help. We have got to put on our thinking caps and figure this out."

They were right. I looked around at the tanning faces of my family and could see the gears in their heads at work. As for me? I could not think of one thing. I was busy watching as the beach filled up with groups of people. Some were young families with brightly colored umbrellas to shade the young ones. Some were teenagers with their boom boxes and Frisbees. Others were dragging several picnic tables together for a reunion. Inner tubes, buckets, balls, shovels, rafts, and food, food, food! It would be a great day at the beach indeed!

It was Charlie's voice that penetrated my thoughts: "I think we need to go back and find out when they discovered Wanderer missing. Maybe that will give us the clues we need to solve this."

"That may explain a few things to me—like why I am having nightmares," Christopher said quietly to himself.

This was one of the few times he talked about those nightmares. We still didn't understand what they were about.

"You are going to have to tell us more about those nightmares one of these days, but right now we have a job to do," Chet stated.

After a little more discussion, it was decided that we would think about the summer after Wanderer was missing.

"My turn to rub Apples' ear!" Emma said as she moved into place.

"I guess it is also my turn, seeing as I got robbed of it last time," said Chet, who actually looked excited as he began to rub her other ear. We all joined hands. "Is everyone ready?" Chet asked.

"Ready," we all replied.

It was that simple: We were all back in time. The scene change was a dramatic one. Where there had been people enjoying a leisurely day at the beach, we now saw the Native Americans silhouetted against the blue sky in the distance as they stood in canoes and fished. I couldn't help but be amazed at the graceful beauty as they kept perfect balance, never losing their footing, but rolling with each wave and ripple.

Farther back into the dunes, people of all ages were working on many different projects, gathering grasses, making clothes or moccasins, and cooking. All the while they seemed to enjoy chatting and laughing. I thought about the many movies I had seen where the Native American people only said, "How," and wondered where anyone had gotten that idea.

A rather large group of children were playing some sort of game with a ball and a stick. Christopher and Charlie both took off in that direction to see if they could join in. Apples, who was always eager to show off her language skills, went along, stating that this time the Odawa would see us and that she wanted to help the boys understand what was being said. This did not take long; I think children understand a universal language all their own, and soon they were laughing with the Odawa. Apples soon returned and took Emma to where a group of girls her age were sitting and playing with babies and toddlers. That was something she would love—babies, lots of babies—and she would forget all about her Barbies for now.

I noticed that many of the adults kept their eyes on the children playing. They smiled at and made comments about the children with such affection and warmth that my own heart swelled with emotion. I looked over at my own children and remembered why we had come. "I should've reminded them why we are here," I said aloud, "otherwise they are going to get so involved with these new friends of theirs they might forget to try to find out what we can do to help."

"Ah would not be so concerned about that if Ah was you," Apples said. "They will continue to learn as they play. Ah always do. Right now, it is time Ah introduce you to them. This won't be so easy, seeing that grown-ups usually have the hardest time just relaxing and letting life happen."

As Apples spoke, her shoulders slumped forward.

I was ready to meet them. I had already met Moon-Deer and was very excited to meet the others. The look on Chet's face showed he was more than ready.

Apples introduced us as "children of the New World." Chet and I both smiled, but they did not. Their faces took on a look of concern, mixed with some hope. We were led into one of the wigwams and introduced to Wanderer's parents. I recognized Moon-Deer, of course, and learned that her husband was Standing-Elk, the tribe's medicine man or priest.

"He has powerful magic and has had a vision that help would come out of the New World someday," Apples explained.She began to interpret for us.

"You are our friends," Standing-Elk explained. "Many footsteps have blown away in the wind, but you have been called to for help, and the wind carried that call to you. Your footsteps have brought you here."

"I am not sure why you need us; you have great power," Chet replied with much respect.

"We have called to many for help," Standing-Elk said. "You alone have come, for you have the gift of a wonderful dog. We have heard her legend. All of us have great gifts and power, but it is not until powers are united that they become truly strong."

Standing-Elk stood as he spoke, then walked over and stroked Apples' head. I could not believe how tall she sat, and that blue eye looked like lightning as it lit up the wigwam. Moon-Deer, too, went over and petted Apples. It was as though they thought she was sacred somehow.

Standing-Elk continued to explain, "My son has gone to the next life; of that we are sure. At first, we thought he had gotten lost, but now we know he is dead. In a vision, Moon-Deer learned from our ancestors and our descendants also that Wanderer has not found the way. This we must do something about; this is why you have come here to help us. There is much you will learn and much you should never forget."

Chet and I looked at each other. We had no idea what we were getting into, but we felt very assured that it would be OK and that we would learn whatever we needed to learn.

We were invited to stay and visit with them a bit longer and learn more of their ways. I was very eager to do this, and I felt free to look around the wigwam as the conversation became lighter.

The room was quite spacious. There was one large door with a deerskin pulled back to let in plenty of light. The floor was hard-packed dirt, swept clean before a fresh layer of pine boughs was laid upon it. All along the wall of this round room was a raised platform that was used as beds and covered with many furs used as blankets. Birch-bark baskets were located at different intervals throughout the room and contained the family members' belongings in them. Above the platform, tools used for hunting and fishing were hung. Right in the center of this cozy home was a place for a fire, and an opening in the wigwam directly above the fire let out any smoke.

I smiled at Moon-Deer, and she giggled. I liked her a lot; we belonged to each other.

We then returned outside with the rest of the tribe. They had gathered to receive some kind of news. Standing-Elk gave them news, but we did not understand it. They all returned to their previous activities. Most of them were getting ready for supper, which was being prepared on outdoor fires.

The children and those who had been hunting or fishing now joined the group. I loved how kind and affectionate the men were to the children. How could these tender, loving men have been called savages?

My own children had come with the others. Immediately, all attention was on Christopher. They were all curious about him and his great likeness to Wanderer. I was told that, except for his clothes, Christopher looked just like Wanderer.

Christopher told them about how he found the snow snake, and he apologized for taking it and disturbing Wanderer's grave.

All was forgiven. After all, Wanderer, who they also called Wind-Traveler, had never been laid to rest.

Standing-Elk then took Chet, me, and our children into the wigwam to show us Wanderer's belongings. He told them that Wanderer had been a fine hunter as he showed them the boy's bow and arrows that hung above what must have been his place on the raised bed. Standing-Elk smiled as he explained that Wanderer had been quite the trickster and spoke with much pride about how much he had loved animals. Standing-Elk then showed them the items in Wanderer's basket, and when they saw the snow snake, they were astonished. They could not believe it was there! It was in very good shape and had symbolic paintings on it that had no longer shown up the first time they'd seen it, but they could tell by the shape it was the same one.

We left before they were going to eat dinner. As we said goodbye, many people came to pet Apples and hug the children.

Standing-Elk and Moon-Deer took our hands and thanked us for our help.

"We know you will find the way," Moon-Deer said with much confidence.

Standing-Elk gave each of us a small leather pouch beautifully decorated with dyed seeds and small shells. "These medicine bags will bring you magic and give you favor with the Great Spirit," he explained.

The usual rub of Apples' ears did not take us back to our time, but to where we could see Eddie furiously digging in the dirt near a white pine's roots.

"Hey, Eddie, what are you doing?" Chet asked. When Eddie did not respond, we knew we had not returned to our current time, but to a time maybe just a few hours or a day before.

He was sweating as he lifted out a square tin box. Sitting cross-legged, he took out a rosary and a cross necklace that he quickly put on. There in the dunes, tears mingled with his sweat as he asked Jesus to forgive him for his April Fools' joke gone wrong. "I don't know how to fix what I did," he mumbled into his sleeve as he wiped the tears from his face.

Emma was the first to say that we needed to help Eddie because he was truly sorry and seemed to have learned a lesson.

"But how?" Christopher asked. He moved closer to Eddie and could see that the money was in the tin box. We watched as Eddie reburied the tin and left for home.

"Dude! The money is still there!" Christopher exclaimed.

Charlie jumped forward, straightening his crooked hat, and asked, "Can we just take it and sneak it back to where it belongs?"

"Yah! Just take the paper and pen out of mah pocket and..." Apples said.

"Your POCKET?" we all asked at once.

"That's what Ah said, 'pocket,' right there in mah biggest spot here on mah hip." Apples gave the spot a lick, and sure enough, there was a pen and paper!

Charlie, with pen in hand, quickly wrote what Chet thought would be best.

Eddie,

All is forgiven. I will make sure the money is returned. Make better choices now, son. Jesus loves you.

Your friend

We made a switch with the note in the tin and the money into Christopher's pocket. Rubbing the dog's ears back to our current time, we traveled without Eddie even knowing we had been there.

By the third day of Vacation Bible School, everyone knew a miracle had happened: The money was replaced. While we all were thanking God for the miracle, Eddie piped up and said, "Jesus! You want to know something about Jesus?" With one finger in the air, he announced: "One, He loves us," and with a second finger added, "two, He forgives sins, and," holding up a third finger, "He is our friend!"

CHAPTER SIX

NOW WHAT?

Saturday was a beautiful day, and we decided that "Apples, Oh, Beautifullest Queen, High Royal Supreme One That Is Loved and Cherished by All" deserved a nice day at the beach, so we headed down to the private beach. "It's about time, Ah would say!" said Apples as her blue eye winked.

I remember thinking, "Oh Lord, there will be no living with her now."

She loved the water. It was still a bit on the cool side, but the hotter days and nights had done a good job of steadily raising the water temperatures up to where we could enjoy it more.

After a quick dip, Chet and I took our spot in our beach chairs to enjoy the sun and some reading.

"Did you notice how dignified and almost majestic the Odawa walked?" Chet asked as he towel-dried his hair and sat beside me.

I had actually been thinking the same thing. "Yes, I did, and with so much grace, too," I said. "I kind of hated having to come back, actually."

Chet looked at me smiling as he brushed some hair away from my face and said, "I don't think they will ever ask us to stay, and I don't blame them. They have all passed to the final journey; we are not ready for that one yet."

"That's true," I said, laughing. "They call themselves the Original People—I like that for them." I sighed.

"Look at meh! Ahm Queen of Dog World!" Apples shouted.

What the heck was she doing now? Standing balancing on an inner tube, yelling her head right off!

All three kids scrambled to shush her up, and Christopher grabbed the inner tube to dump her off. Charlie threw a Frisbee her way, hoping she would fill her loud mouth with it, and Emma, hoping to fool anyone around, pretended like she was doing the yelling and hollered, "Ahm Queen of Dogs!"

"Ahm dive in, WOO-HOO!" Apples yelled. *Splash!*

"Oh my gosh, is she actually doing the backstroke?" I gasped.

"I'm not sure, but did you know your dog can talk?" Eddie said around a mouthful of a half-eaten peanut butter and jelly sandwich.

How long had Eddie been sitting there? Chet and I could only look at him and blink! One thing we did know was that the sandwich he was eating was definitely the one that was supposed to be for Apples.

"Ahm don't care! Ah wish Ah could have seen your faces! WAA-waa-WAA-HAA!"

"Oh, stop." Getting back to the story....

Finally, Chet asked, "Are you sure that it wasn't Emma talking?"

"Yep, pretty darn sure," Eddie said as he licked the last of the jelly from his short black thumb and ran into the water to join the kids.

"Tell the readers Ah was good when he kept trying to make meh talk! Ah didn't, did Ah? Ah was a good dog."

"You were trying, but it was a bit late for that. It helped a lot that Emma just kept answering in your voice."

The rest of the afternoon went off without incident, and before we realized it, it was time to pack it up and get ready to go to the Muldunes' for dinner. Sighing with relief, I said goodbye to Eddie, but I did wonder what he believed about our family and the dog.

We all enjoyed the Muldunes. Sarah and Al had three children the same ages as mine. Danny was twelve, Kevin was eleven, and their daughter, Katie, was seven, the same as Emma. This made for some pretty good times shared by our two families.

Al was a hamburger master—he made the best and biggest hamburgers in the world! He made them as big as pizzas and had to specially order big, round buns from the local bakery. Al's burgers were true works of art. After cutting them into wedges and serving a wedge to each of us, we were instructed to "top 'em the way you like 'em!"

Sarah always set out a table loaded with amazing toppings: ketchup, mustard, pickles, onions, three kinds of cheese, mayo, crisp bacon, lettuce, tomatoes, sautéed mushrooms, and guacamole! All those yummy toppings—and Al only put ketchup and a slice of American cheese on his. "The way a true hamburger lover eats 'em," he always said before his first huge bite. The rest of us loaded up on all the goodies, each claiming that ours was the way a true hamburger lover *really* eats them.

"We just know where to go for great food," Chet said, laughing.

"What do you think our Odawa friends put on their burgers?" Emma asked. Then she added, "We can ask them the next time we go back in time."

If what she had said to the Muldunes was strange to them, I'm sure that our reaction was far stranger. We just sat there for the second time that day with our mouths hanging open, not knowing what to do or say, and blinked at her.

"That is why Ahm always telling you to take meh along," Apples said. *"Ah would have said something like, 'Oh? Are you going on another one of your little trips, kiddo? Maybe you ought to pack a real suitcase this time.' But no, you couldn't think of that one, could you? Or how about this one: 'Next time, send a postcard—we would love to see where you say you have been sometime.' You have got to stop leaving meh at home; Ah could whisper some of mah best lines to you."*

"Apples, we would not want to say any of that to Emma," I said. *"It may make her look or feel like a fool in front of people. After all, she was not making any of it up. She just said something she should not have. Now, if you are finished with yet another interruption, I will continue."*

It was Kevin who saved us all a lot of embarrassment by yelling, "Yeah! Let's all be Odawa and return to that time!"

"So, you see, you were not needed at all. I know these things shock you, but that's the way it goes."

"Well, Ah still like mah idea better, and so do mah fans and readers!"

"Apples..."

Anyway, off they ran to play Odawa for a couple of hours. Needless to say, we did have to promise each other to be a bit more careful in the future about what we said in front of others. So, that evening after saying thank-yous and goodbyes to the Muldunes, we made a pact to only speak of time-traveling at home when we were alone.

I remember wondering if we should really even be getting into this—and then Christopher had his next nightmare.

"Help! Someone, please help!" The cries in the night were from the boys' room. We were all at Christopher's side in a minute. Charlie was already shaking him awake and Emma was rubbing the sleep from her eyes when Chet and I arrived.

A very shaken Christopher said, "I dreamed again that I was drowning and so cold. I'm freezing. It is so real! I could see people, but they could not see or hear me. I was so scared! The people were Odawa, Mom!"

He even felt cold. Apples decided that she would sleep with him the rest of the night. This always helped when one of the children was sick or had just had a bad day. It didn't bring me much comfort, though. I was really beginning to be concerned for the safety of my kids. We had never had trouble with nightmares before. Now it seemed they were happening more often. Christopher had two the week before and had them every night that week, and every night they seemed to be worse. At first, he could barely remember them, but now these dreams had more detail and even affected his body temperature.

I felt a bit frightened as I asked Chet, "What if the Odawa want Christopher to replace Wanderer? We have to do something about this. We cannot have our kids suffering from nightmares and blurting out things about time-traveling with a dog, of all things. Maybe we should not get so involved with this. We really don't know what we are doing at all!"

The one thing that was a bit reassuring was that Apples' brown eye, the one that warned of danger, was calm. I guess I was learning to trust Apples a little bit through all of this.

"Yeah, and it was about time, too. You were the slowest at learning this out of everyone Ah had ever known. It took every persuasive power Ah had to convince you to trust meh!"

"Well, actually, I put my trust in our Heavenly Father—and still in all, we had made a promise."

The last two weeks of July were just as busy as the month had started. Both the annual sand sculpting contest and the volleyball tournaments were held that month. We always built a sand sculpture and entered it in the family category, but we lost the previous two years to the Muldunes. Last year they made a huge family hamburger, complete with ketchup and pickles by using food coloring to dye some sand red and green, and the year before that they had made a snowman!

Our chances were looking very good this year because Apples started digging up a big pile of sand for us, and soon Christopher, Charlie, and Emma had it looking just like a wigwam. Chet had the food coloring and was adding dyed bits of sand that looked like the beadwork that adorned the Odawa wigwams.

Emma found a few twigs that, when put into the top of the wigwams, looked just like the branches the birch bark had been laid across. Christopher carved a snow snake, a drum, and a dog down one side, and Charlie collected up small sticks to press into the sides to resemble the pine root stitching we had seen. We all decorated it with small stones and shells.

"I wish Moon-Deer and Standing-Elk could see this!" Christopher said as he stood brushing sand from his hands and knees.

"I am pretty sure they would be very proud of the influence they have had on us, for sure," Chet said, agreeing.

And what do you know? It was then announced that the five of us had just taken first place for our sand sculpture in the family category!

"Uhm … can't you count? Ah was there, too, you know, and Ah made the pile of sand for you—Ah deserve some credit! Ah deserve to be counted as a family member, too."

Apples was right; she sure did!

Before we knew it, two weeks had passed since our last travel through time, and we still had not thought up one good solution to the problem the Odawa had. We walked Apples every day but had not even been summoned. It took us all awhile to wrap our heads around time-traveling because, for us, it had been two weeks in what we called "real time," or our time, but in the world of time-traveling, time did not really exist—at least that was Chet's theory. He said it wasn't as if the Odawa were standing around waiting for us, either.

Our yearly camping vacation was just three days away, so maybe a change of scenery and rested minds would help us come up with the right answers for Moon-Deer and Standing-Elk—and, oh my gosh, what about Wanderer? What had it been like for him? Even though I still had moments of concern for my own kids, I was still resolved to find that boy!

So, the first week in August, we headed up into the Porcupine Mountains for camping. Aside from the fact that the campground was a beautiful park, they also offered tons of activities for kids: horseback riding, canoeing, swimming, hiking, scavenger hunts, hayrides, and arts and crafts. The camp had a nature center full of information about Lake Michigan and the surrounding dunes. Ranger Rick hosted hiking expeditions and classes to introduce children to insects, plants, and animals that lived in the dunes. They also had an organized club kids could join the week of their stay. If either Chet or I had any hopes of getting the kids' thoughts off Native Americans that week, we were sorely mistaken. The club that was offered was none other than "Life with the Potawatomi, Chippewa, and Odawa: The Three Fires." All three of them wasted no time in signing up!

We hadn't even left for camp yet! Nope, there was no way we were going to get Native Americans out of their heads at all.

"Ah knew this would happen," Apples said. "Ah had it planned from the beginning. Ah love it when mah plans work out so well!" She couldn't help prancing.

"How do you figure this was your plan? You were not included in the planning," I reminded her.

"You would not believe meh if Ah told you, but to prove it," she then sat, "Ah will tell you this: Ah was on a mission—that's it, a mission. Ah planned the whole adventure mahself. It was mah idea to be there and mah idea to meet Mr. Butz."

"Not thinking that proves anything," I said, "but you do crack me up. The only thing I believe you had a hand—or should I say, 'paw'—in was picking out Mr. Butz's native name for him. Who else would call him Bear? Little Bear Butz!"

"Now Ah ahm truly insulted! Of course Ah had no paw in that!!" Apples said. "It will be quite a while before Ah ever tell you anything again—ever!"

"Nice," I replied, "maybe I can get to the end of this story."

I think I was telling you about the kids joining the Three Fires club that was led by Mr. Little Bear Butz and how they were looking forward to the first meeting at 10 a.m. Monday. Two whole days to wait. Two whole days for Chet and I to wonder if this would cause Christopher's nightmares to worsen or to possibly be forgotten altogether.

CHAPTER SEVEN

CAMPING

We spent the first day setting up camp: deciding which tree was best to lean the bikes on and which one was best to keep Apples tied to, where to put a clothesline, the best spot for inner tubes, where exactly to put up the screen tent and outdoor kitchen area—was it too close or too far from the firepit?—where to put the lawn chairs, and who wanted to string up our crazy "hot dogs in a bun" patio lights. The trailer, stocked with enough goodies to last a month, stood between two pines.

"These are white pines," Charlie informed us. "See, if you pull out the needles, they come out in groups of five, representing W-H-I-T-E. And, of course, these are silver birch," he said, pointing to about four trees standing behind the trailer a bit. "The rest of these are oak," he finished. We were all impressed.

Our firepit was just a little off-center in the clearing, so we put the screen tent on the opposite side of the trailer. The picnic tables and coolers were arranged on the inside of it. The clothesline was then run from three smaller oaks that were just in back of the screen tent, and Apples would have the tree closest to the firepit to herself.

She really didn't need a leash because she stayed with us like a very good dog, but leashing your dog was a camp rule, so we at least had the leash—just in case.

The best place for the inner tubes was to lean them at the front of the trailer. Lawn chairs, of course, were arranged around the firepit to make wiener and marshmallow roasting convenient. All of this planning and placing took time, but soon we were ready for our week of camping.

With the work done, we were ready to eat. Steaks cooked over the grill were on the menu for the first night.

"Mom, can I have the biggest and the juiciest one?" Charlie asked. He always wanted the biggest, juiciest one.

"What if the biggest is the driest?" Chet was asking as Christopher inquired, "What if the third smallest is the juiciest?"

Emma didn't have much to say about it, as she preferred hot dogs any day. She and I were busy wrapping potatoes and corn on the cob in foil. We would eat well before exploring our surroundings by bike.

"This is exactly what the world smelled like in Wanderer's days," Christopher said as he drew in a deep breath with his arms out to the sides.

The smell of pine mingled with the smell of wood burning was what he was referring to. We had all been sitting and gazing into the fire for a few minutes after we had eaten.

"You know, I think you are right about that," Chet replied, then added, "and I am sure that good Odawa helped with cleanup, so let's get at it and get it done and on with our bike rides."

We were not the only family that had planned an evening bike ride. The family on the next site was leaving for a ride the same time as we were. We learned that they were Harry and Nancy Jones. They and their twelve-year-old daughter, Laura, were from the Detroit area. They all had blonde hair and blue-green eyes, and I remember thinking I had never seen a husband and wife look so much alike in my life! Laura was one of the cutest girls I had ever seen; her light gold freckles and the small space between her two front teeth gave her a lot of charm. I think Christopher was falling in love, or at least like, but he would never admit to that. Laura was telling us about some of the other campers with kids and some of the activities she had signed up for as we rode along. She had been there for four days already, so she knew quite a bit about it. As the children talked among themselves, Harry took over the conversation among us adults. He was a firefighter. As he spoke, I noticed that Nancy grew quiet and seemed annoyed with Harry. I had a feeling that listening to one firefighter story after another had become routine for Nancy. Maybe I was wrong, and maybe she was just concerned for him. After all, he did have a very dangerous job.

We were entering a slightly darkened path into shade trees when we noticed a man stripping some bark off a silver birch tree.

"Why is that guy doing that?" Charlie wanted to know.

"I hope you're not asking me, because I have no idea," I answered.

We had stopped to watch him when Nancy asked, "Laura, isn't that your club leader, Little Bear Butz?"

"Yes, that is him! I wonder what he is doing," Laura said, very curious. "We could ask him or just watch him for a little while longer!"

"I vote we just leave him alone; you kids can ask him about it later," Chet said. "I don't think he would appreciate us spying on him."

I agreed and added, "It probably has something to do with the club you will be going to on Monday morning."

As we left the wooded area, we could hear him singing in a Native American dialect.

"This guy is for real, isn't he," Christopher stated instead of asked.

"He sure is," Laura informed him. "He is the most 'for real' Native American guy I ever met."

"How many Native Americans have you met, anyway?" Nancy asked, laughing. For the first time that evening she didn't look tired. Turning to me, she said, "Laura loves the Three Fires club more than anything else here. She could talk about it for hours if we'd let her."

I knew we were not going to let her because Harry had already changed the subject to firefighting. Nancy had grown quiet again.

This time I knew why. The only thing Harry *ever* talked about was firefighting. Poor Nancy.

Chet and I exchanged a look of disbelief when Harry called over to some very astonished campers to say, "You know you have that fire burning way too high, don't you?" He then decided to stop at their site and tell them all he knew about fires. Nancy smiled apologetically.

Poor Nancy, I thought again.

The kids were all off racing to see who would be the first back to camp.

"Laura won!" Emma yelled, then followed that with a big: "YAY for the girls!"

"Yay for the girls!" Nancy and I yelled in unison.

We had all gone our separate ways, and soon we had a pretty good fire roaring ourselves. We had just about eaten our fill of s'mores when we saw Harry return to his camp. We watched as he tried several different methods to build a fire on his own site, and a few minutes later he came over and asked if he and his family could join ours.

"Better at stopping them than starting them," he laughed heartily—except he was the only one laughing. We spent the rest of the evening listening (or trying to listen) to Harry's stories.

"Ah hate it when we have company and Ah cannot talk," Apples said as soon as they were out of sight. "Ah could have added quite a bit to the conversation, you know. Ah remember many a time mah own life was in danger as Ah fought fires. Especially the Great Chicago Fire. To this day Ah do not trust cows. Can you blame meh?"

"I know, but I am very proud of you for keeping quiet. I know what a struggle that can be for you," I said, patting her head and giving her a dog cookie. "Maybe Eddie taught you a lesson."

"Well, then, can Ah have a peanuttier-buttery one? Ah just love peanuttier-buttery ones," Apples said. We all laughed like we always did when she said that.

"Two cookies for the dog, then to bed we go," Chet said with a stretch and a yawn.

We had just settled ourselves in for the night when someone—well, I think it was about ten someones—began singing.

"There was a farmer who had a dog and Bingo was his name-o!" they sang for over an hour. At that point, Chet asked sarcastically, "Don't you just *love* camping?"

"Ah do not know about camping," Apples said. "Ah ahm still trying to figure out who the heck this Bing-o is. Ah do not recall a subject of mine with the name Bing-o."

"I always thought the *farmer's* name was Bingo!" Emma stated with raised eyebrows and wide eyes.

"Yah, that makes more sense to meh," Apples said, closing her eyes as her head lowered to her outstretched paws.

We all laughed at that—and with a *B-I-N-G-O! B-I-N-G-O! B-I-N-G-O!*—we finally went to *SLEEP-O!*

Nothing is better than waking up to the smell of bacon frying in the good outdoors, not to mention coffee! I was really glad that Chet had gotten up early and had breakfast going.

After breakfast and a few cleanup chores, the kids rode off to check the day's activity board. They hoped it would be either canoeing or a hayride. Whatever it ended up being, I knew it would keep their minds off the Three Fires club a little bit longer and their bodies occupied. At least until noon anyway!

With the exception of Charlie somehow managing to fall out of his canoe, the morning had been a success, seeing that fun was the goal. After a hearty lunch and playing with and walking the dog, they decided to get in touch with Laura, whose dad was giving her a fire drill complete with red fire hat and everything! They asked her if she would like to go to the beach with us later that afternoon. She was delighted. The day had become very hot, and a refreshing dip sounded great. Her parents did not like the beach because of the hot, itchy sand. I thought to myself that Harry probably didn't like sand because it wouldn't burn, and if it did, it was too close to the water, making it too easy to put out! I had to admit, though, if ever my house was on fire, I would sure want someone as dedicated as Harry to show up.

The kids, who were already tanned, were getting darker every day. As they all played in the waves, I marveled that none of them had come back to our blanket once for a snack. I knew they were really working up appetites today.

Soon they were having a sandcastle contest. They worked as individuals for a while but then joined their separate castles into one big one, complete with bridges made of bark that Laura added and moats Christopher dug with care.

Emma collected stones and packed them into all sides.

Christopher exclaimed, "It looks like it's built entirely of rocks!"

Charlie placed pieces of driftwood to look like knights in armor guarding the castle. I made a mental note for next year's sand sculpture contest back home.

Charlie was the first one to realize how hungry he was and came over looking for chips and a drink. "You know what, Mom?" he said through smacking lips. "When we are done helping Wanderer, we should go back to the Middle Ages and meet knights and damsels in distress."

Yikes! I thought, Then, with relief, I remembered that someone would have to summon our help to do that, and I was already praying that no one would!

Seeing Charlie chowing down made the rest of them realize that he wasn't the only hungry kid in the world. They had gotten cases of the munchies, too.

The sound of the waves and gulls and other kids playing in the distance could hardly be heard over the smacking, crunching, and talking with full mouth noises at our blanket.

"Hey, that is awesome," Christopher said, pointing at the ankle bracelet Laura was wearing. We all thought it was interesting. The charm was a circle with threads wrapped around it so that the center looked like a web. A small feather and some beads hung from the outside of this, and then it was tied to her ankle with a single strip of leather.

"What does the charm symbolize, if you don't mind me asking?" Chet said.

"Oh, this is a dream catcher," Laura replied. "Bear said Native Americans used them to trap bad dreams in and only good dreams can get through the netting to the dreamer. Native

Americans are my hobby, sort of; I read anything I can to learn more about them. I wish I was Native American."

Christopher was about ready to burst. "Yeah, Native Americans are my hobby, too, you could say! But does it work? The dream catcher, I mean."

Laura laughed out loud. "Of course it works," she said. "Why? Have you been seeing monsters in your dreams?"

"Not monsters exactly, but bad dreams plenty," Christopher replied, his cheeks burning red.

"I hate to be the one to point this out to you, Chet, but I think the kids might make us move into a wigwam after this summer!" I said, taking off my sunglasses so I could see his expression.

He did not look the least bit concerned as he replied, "Oh, I think everything will work out fine. Look, she is giving him her dream catcher."

"First a dream catcher, then a wigwam!" I said, laughing.

The rest of the afternoon was spent sharing what information they all had about Native Americans with one another.

What in the world was the rest of this week going to be like? I wondered.

CHAPTER EIGHT

THREE FIRES CLUB

The kids were all up before Chet and I were on Monday morning. By eight o'clock they had eaten bowls of cereal for breakfast, gotten cleaned up and dressed, and were ready to go.

"You know what, Mom?" Christopher didn't wait for me to ask *what* as he continued, "The dream catcher really works! I actually had a very cool dream last night. I was with all the Odawa and having a great time. I was not afraid once!" His eyes couldn't have been brighter. I was glad for that.

"Well, Ah ahm not surprised one bit! We should have gone back and told Moon-Deer and Standing-Elk about the nightmares from the beginning, but NO! nobody wanted to trust mah beautiful blue eye," Apples said, standing with one paw propped on the picnic table and the other raised up alongside her head as she spoke.

Chet walked over and moved her paw from the table to the ground as he said, "One night without a nightmare does not prove anything. It is a good start, but we would like more reliable results."

Apples was getting that know-it-all look on her face when Laura arrived, excited and ready for the club.

"Let me guess, no nightmares last night, right?" Laura asked.

Christopher nodded as his long lashes grazed his blushing cheeks.

"I told you, it works like a charm," she said, smiling.

"Ah knew Ah liked this kid!" Apples' voice rang out for all to hear.

"Who said that?" Laura's brow wrinkled.

"Who said what?" all five of us choked out.

"Never mind. Are you ready?" she asked.

Yes, they were ready. After goodbyes were said over shoulders, they were gone.

"Sorry about that, Ah forgot," Apples said. "Ah cannot help it if Ah forget things now and again. It would help if she looked more like that Eddie kid! Ahm only a dog, you know!"

It was very convenient for Apples to sometimes be "only a dog."

I was glad she took such a long nap that morning, and I hoped that after such a close call, she would remember to be more careful with her blabbing when the kids returned later.

I needn't have worried, though. When they returned, they had so much to share that she couldn't have fit in a word in edgewise anyway!

"We met Mr. Bear Butz!" Emma said. "We can call him Mr. Bear or Mr. Butz." She pointed her finger, "But he thinks Bear Butz is just silly!"

"We learned about the Anishinabek, the people of this place," Christopher started out by saying.

"Mr. Bear is Odawa, too!" Charlie jumped in.

"Odawa means 'one who makes pictographs,'" Emma added.

Christopher finished with: "He showed us how to do it, too!"

"Remember when we saw him in the woods getting birch bark? That is what we used for the pictographs," Charlie said, now on a roll. "We told him we saw him and heard him singing to thank the spirit of the tree for the gift of the bark."

"Isn't it totally cool? Look at the design in mine," Emma said, holding up her artwork.

As they each held theirs up, Chet and I were impressed at how unique each one was and admired all three of them as they explained how the designs were created.

"These marks are made by biting the bark," Christopher said. "We used our teeth to create our own personal art. That is how the Odawa got their tribal name!"

"I remember seeing pieces like these in Standing-Elk's wigwam and on some of the other wigwams in the village," Chet said.

"Mr. Bear liked us, too," Emma stated.

"Yeah, he really liked our medicine bags," Christopher said as he removed his from his pocket.

"Uh-oh," said Apples as her brown eye rolled slightly.

"Uh-oh," I agreed. "Do you think he realized that they were the real thing?" I asked no one in particular.

"Do you think you would recognize your own face in the mirror? Of course he knows it is the real thing!" Apples looked as smug as she possibly could.

"Did he ask anything in particular about them or just mention that they were nice bags?" I asked Christopher.

"He just said we must have some mighty powerful gifts to have bags like this," Christopher said. Then he added, "We told him a friend gave them to us, and he did not say anything else about them. Did we do something wrong?"

"It is not really wrong," Apples answered. Her eye had already calmed down. "He probably believes a friend gave them to you. Ah personally don't understand why you all just cannot tell the world that the Queen of Dog World lives with you and now you all can time travel. Ahm sure that Mr. Butz would be fascinated by the whole thing."

"Yes, I am sure he would—and so would the media, so no thanks," Chet said with finality.

With the exception that Harry said Laura's pictograph was a fire hazard and made her put it in the car, the day was a fairly normal one. It was not until after swimming, hiking, and dinner that the other shoe—I mean, moccasin—was dropped.

We were taking turns telling ghost stories around the fire that night when Mr. Bear stopped by. I was not at all surprised by this, and Chet was glad to meet him. They hit it off right away.

Apples liked him right away, too. She had moved from where she was lying close to the fire to be next to him. He was petting her when he asked if we had heard the Native American legend of the dog. I couldn't believe there was a story or legend having to do with dogs that she had not already told us several times.

"The dog has the least of powers," Bear started saying. "He is not fast like a fox and is weaker than a wolf. He is not as smart as a mink and very clumsy compared to the grace of the deer."

As he spoke, I was having a hard time not laughing at what I knew Apples would want to say: *Unless you are the queen!* or *Ah ahm queen!*

"The dog felt as if he had no gifts and nothing to offer," Little Bear continued. "He wanted to do something, so he pledged his love to man. From the beginning of time, the dog has not left the side of man."

"Thank you for sharing that story," I said. "We feel privileged that you share your heritage with us."

"I have only given to you what is yours," Little Bear replied. "You, too, are of the same heritage, or you would not have been given the medicine bags. It is not for me to know where you have gotten them or why. If there is any help I can give you, I offer it now. There is power in the bags, and they give you favor with the Great Spirit. That is all I need to know."

And with that, he stood and said goodbye.

"Ah love the part about dogs giving their love to man the best. It is true: Many, many, many of mah friends love the Odawa, and they are loved right back. They understood that some of us could talk and that queens could time travel and that we should be able to go to the ice-cream parlor—"

"Apples—"

"—and sit on the furniture—"

"Apples—"

"—and drive the jeep!"

"Drive the jeep?! Are you crazy? Just let me get on with the story, OK?"

"OK, but it is a good thing Ah love you."

CHAPTER NINE

MR. BEAR BUTZ

Each day at camp was a little like the day before. The kids came back from the Three Fires club full of newly learned facts and learned many things about nature from Ranger Rick. We did the usual swimming, riding bikes, and relaxing, had good food, and listened to more firefighter stories than we could stand.

The *B-I-N-G-O* people sang every night the whole time we were there, but we did not hear of any more nightmares. The nightmares seemed to have ended. The Joneses had to leave on our fifth day at camp. The four kids made promises to keep in touch. They had planned a Native American club of their own and decided pen pals would be the best way to continue sharing new information.

"If your friend could give you another medicine bag for me, I would really like to have one," Laura said as she waved from the back seat of the car.

"When I see him again, I will ask him," promised Christopher.

We all waved goodbye as Harry pulled away, his head hanging out the open window, making a fire siren sound as loud as his lungs allowed.

"Poor Nancy," I sighed.

"We are going to have to leave before too long, too," Christopher commented as he watched Charlie toss a ball around for Apples.

I could tell he was thinking about something when he said, "Maybe we should let Mr. Bear help us. He might know what to do."

"I wish that we could, but I really wouldn't even know what to ask," I said.

"I think the hardest part would be how we are going to explain how we got into this—or even how we got the snow snake," Chet added.

"He wouldn't want to know how we got the snow snake. He might understand something about it that I don't," Christopher explained.

"I have a feeling you might be right. Let's think about it awhile," Chet decided.

I had a feeling that Little Bear might show up at our campfire that night, so I figured we had better think about it right then!

I was right—he did show up.

"We've been expecting you," Chet said, laughing.

"It is the work of the medicine bag," he explained. "It has brought us together. It will continue to bring friends and help into your path. I am the son of a medicine man; I understand its power. Apparently, someone has put much trust in you."

"Yes, that is about the size of things," Chet said. "We have been entrusted with this—mission, so to speak, and we all feel a bit incapable to carry it out at times."

Mr. Bear looked very understanding, then asked, "Have you been given anything else?"

At first, we all just looked at one another. Then we looked at Apples, and her blue eye was winking and blinking, so I said, "Yes, they gave Christopher something that had belonged to their son."

Bear asked if we had it here with us and if he could see it, so Christopher brought it out. Little Bear knew what it was right away.

"A snow snake? My people played with these all winter long," he said, smiling. As he took it from Christopher, his smile faded. "There is much sorrow in this." He looked confused and said, "This should have been buried with their son."

"We didn't tell you he was dead," Christopher said flatly.

"He would be dead by now," Bear said gently. "Boys today do not play with snow snakes. There is much sadness, a loss of some kind. I could tell you more, but I feel you know more than I do. I do know something, though, something that will help. Tomorrow at Three Fires I will teach you."

It was not long after that that we called it a night. After Mr. Butz had left, I said, "Everyone thinks we will figure this out but me, I guess."

"And me," Chet replied.

"Do you think Mr. Bear has it figured out?" asked Charlie.

"No, but I think he knows he was sent to teach us something we need to know. Basically, that is what he said," Chet reminded us as he turned out the lights.

Christopher was the first one up the next morning and was busy writing something down when I got up.

"Mom, you know I haven't had a nightmare all week, right?" he said. "But I have been dreaming. The dreams and the nightmares do tie in somehow—they mean something. They are always in my head. I thought if I wrote them down, I might see the connection." As he spoke, the others had joined us.

"Tell us your dreams, and maybe we can help figure it out," Charlie said.

"Well, in one dream I am with other boys playing with the snow snake," Christopher said. "We are having a good time, but then all of a sudden, I realize I am all alone. The others have gone off in different directions. I keep sliding the snow snake along the ice. Then I hear someone that I cannot see say, 'Wind-Traveler, your journey will take you far, for this is your greatest gift and ability.' Then I wake up."

"I can see how they are connected," said Chet, who had just gotten a cup of coffee. "In the nightmare, you are drowning and very cold. In the dream, you are playing along what could be a frozen river or stream."

The realization hit us all at the same time.

"How awful!" I said. "Don't tell me Wanderer drowned while playing with that snow snake! No wonder you had nightmares! You sleep with that thing under your pillow!"

Now we knew what happened to Wanderer: He had fallen through the ice, drowned, and most likely went with the river's current, never to be seen again. His friends or family must have found the snow snake along the shore and placed it in the grave we found.

"Ah had that figured out from the beginning; however, Ah wanted you all to figure it out on your own," Apples said.

"Apples, I do not believe you this time for sure," Chet said. "It is more your style to show off all you know rather than patiently wait for us to figure anything out."

Chet was already frying bacon, and its delicious smell was getting the better of Apples. "OK, Ah admit it. Ah did kind of make that one up. Now can Ah have fourteen slices of bacon and four eggs?" As she spoke, she actually drooled, something Dalmatians rarely do.

"Well, now we know how to make you tell the truth," Christopher laughed as he rubbed her chest.

"Bacon-eating dog," said Charlie, whose sideways hat now had a feather in it, as he began to fill his own plate. The bacon was working on the rest of us too. We were all ready for breakfast.

"You forgot to tell them that Ah only got three slices of bacon and one egg."

"I did not forget; I just don't think it is very important to the story."

"Well, it is important to meh! Ah never get what Ah deserve around here, and the readers need to know how hard it is to be a dog."

"Oh, for Pete's sake, all right. It is hard to be a dog, but it's even harder to write with all these crazy interruptions, so now we are even!"

"Nope, we are not. You are still not a queen."

"Oh, brother! We still are not sure you are a queen!"

After breakfast the boys decided to write down a list of all the facts that they could remember from learning about Native Americans. So far, they had:

1. Native Americans moved often during a year.

2. Summer travel was by foot or canoe.

3. Winter travel was on sleds or toboggans, and they wore snowshoes.

4. They took their wigwams along by rolling them up and packing them into canoes or onto sleds.

5. In spring they headed to maple tree groves to make sugar from the sap.

6. Summer was spent along lakesides where berries could be collected.

7. In the fall they traveled to shallower lakes to gather wild rice.

8. Year-round, they hunted and fished.

9. All the tools they used were handmade by them.

It wasn't until we saw this all written down that we realized they had migrated so much.

"Are Moon-Deer and Standing-Elk still going to be in the same place when we return to help them?" Charlie asked urgently.

All three children looked at us with the same question on their faces.

"Good question," was the only thing Chet or I could think of to say.

"Hey! We are going to be late for Three Fires if we don't leave now," Emma said as she jumped to her feet. With the slam of the trailer door, they were gone!

Chet and I looked over the list again. "There is just so much we do not know," he said, and I sighed in agreement.

The last meeting of Three Fires had begun, and the three kids were sure that it would be the most important one. Charlie had taken a pencil and paper along, and it turns out that was a very wise move.

"Today we will be discussing the funeral customs for Native Americans and the beliefs that would take them into their final journey," Mr. Bear had begun.

Charlie wrote almost word for word what he learned that day. The other two could add anything he missed later.

Mr. Bear realized that this was the last meeting he would have with them also. He gave them each a beaded bracelet that he had made for them.

"I really enjoyed having you in the club this week," he said. "Tell your parents I will drop by later to say goodbye to them also."

With that, the last meeting came to an end. When I saw the three long faces that returned from the meeting, I was glad I had seen a sign-up sheet for a scavenger hunt and signed them up for it.

"Who would like to go to a scavenger hunt tonight?" I asked. Three "I dos" and one "Not meh" rang out. *Good*, I thought, *now we all had something to look forward to and maybe something that would make the last night of camp cheerier.*

The camp offered a five-dollar prize to the first to collect everything on the list. At least the hunt kept them and the other kids at camp occupied for a couple of hours. They ran from tents to trailers collecting bottle caps, sandwich bags, twisty ties, matchbooks, used candles, popsicle sticks, charcoal, and gum wrappers.

I spent the evening handing out what I had to several kids who had come begging from us.

"This is like Halloween in a way," I said to Chet, who was making some hobo pies at the fireside.

"But the costumes are more hilarious here. Did you see that one kid?" said Apples, who had not taken her eyes off the hobo pies.

"Apples, nobody was in costume—where do you come up with this stuff? You sure are a funny dog sometimes," I said, laughing.

"Yep, she is funny, all right," Chet said. "If it wasn't so dark out, you could see me laughing."

"Mom, Dad, we won! We won the five-dollar prize!" yelled Charlie, who was waving the five-dollar bill around in the air as the three of them filled us in. It was hard to follow who was saying what, but it went something like this: They thought their chances of winning would be better if they split the list among them and split up to collect the items needed.

"Sounds like a good plan to me," Chet said. "So, what are your plans for this five-dollar prize?"

Christopher was explaining that they wanted to donate it to the Three Fires club. Soon Mr. Butz arrived, so they quickly changed the subject so the donation would be a surprise for him.

After the usual greetings and some hobo pie, he began, "I came to thank you all for making this summer such an interesting one. I realized from the beginning that you were all on some kind of adventure, and I have enjoyed being a small part of it." Turning to the kids, he asked, "Have you told your parents about today's meeting?"

"Yes, they have," Chet answered. "They took notes, and the information was very interesting to us. We feel that the more we understand, the more our chances to help increase."

I really wanted to know something once and for all, so I just plain got to the point, slightly amused. "How much of our adventure do you know? I have a feeling you know a lot more than you say."

I was not surprised by his answer. "You are right, there are things about this that I know, yet there is much I do not understand," he said. "I can tell you that it is not unusual for my people to see visions or to be visited by our ancestors, or even to be given gifts such as your medicine bags. What I do not understand is—how? How have you been given vision without teaching? I am not going to ask you how; I feel I do not need to know."

We were all listening, taking in each move Bear made with our eyes. The firelight was playing across each face as the shadows flicked about them. We were all spellbound by Bear, the smell of the campfire, and the whisper of the breeze through pines.

He continued speaking. "I know, too, that what you have come to learn, I taught today."

Christopher was the first one with a question. "You mean—we have it?" he asked. "We should be able to do it now?"

Charlie had to finish chewing and swallow his too-big bite of pie before he could ask, "When are we going to do it, then?"

Emma's only contribution to the conversation was to say that she didn't get it. She was not the only one; none of the rest of us had figured it out yet. But we all felt a lot more confident that we would. After all, we were all smart, and Bear had a lot of faith in us.

Before he left, Bear rubbed Apples for a few minutes and said, "It is common among my elders to be given guidance from creatures with the gift of speech."

"WAA-waa-WAA-HAA! See, Ah told you he knew!" Apples said, slapping what I think would be her knee if she had one.

Nevertheless, it had been a very special week of camping, and we were all sorry to have it come to an end.

The wind picked up as we settled in, and it rained all night. The thunder rolled and shook the trailer as the rain pelted the roof and sides. Christopher was not the only one who dreamt that night. We all dreamed that the thunder was the drums of the Odawa and that the rain was their dance. Moon-Deer and Standing-Elk led, and they all danced and danced as they prayed for the return of their son and friend.

When we awoke, none of us was sure that it had been a dream at all.

CHAPTER TEN

HIJACKED

It seemed we missed some excitement at home while we were away camping. As we sat enjoying a glass of iced tea, Sarah Muldune filled us in on what we had missed.

"You know Eddie Daniels, don't you?" she asked.

Oh boy, did we ever! "Yep, we know Eddie!" I nodded.

"Well," Sarah continued, "you know how he is known for his practical jokes and for always playing jokes on everybody? Last Thursday his joke backfired on him. He had told Danny and Kevin to meet him up on the Louie Hill trails at ten o'clock that morning. They had initially agreed to meet him, but forgot they had to go to the dentist. So, of course, they did not show.

"The poor boy had been up on the trail the day before and found a deep hole off the side of a trail," she said. "He thought it would be absolutely hilarious to stick his leg in the hole and pretend like it just fell off somewhere and that now he could no longer walk. Well, Beulah, his poor grandma, began to get really worried around one o'clock when he hadn't shown up for lunch. She looked for him herself for a while, then had the neighbor kids help her. By five o'clock the whole town was looking for him. You can imagine how she felt by then—I mean, what can be worse than not knowing where your child is?"

I knew she wasn't really expecting us to answer that question, but we all looked at each other and somehow knew that this was a reminder of what our mission was all about.

There was more to the story. Sarah continued as we all listened. "The police were called, and when some of the older kids were asked about Eddie, they said they had seen him earlier that day up near Louie Hill trails. When we realized what was going on, Kevin and Danny told the police that they were supposed to meet him up there that morning, too, so maybe he was still there!

"Of course, we all headed up the trails, it was getting dark, and the more people there were looking for him, the better our chances of finding him would be," Sarah said. "We could hear him way before we could see him, although I, for one, didn't think what we were hearing was even human! None of us could even imagine what was making him yell like he was—it was literally a 'scroar': He would roar like a caged animal and scream like a trapped fox. When we finally got to him, his head was almost flipped back like a Pez dispenser, mouth wide open to the sky just to let all the noise out! We all had flashlights and water, and luckily, someone had a first aid kit.

"Eddie had one leg stuck up to his thigh in that hole, with his other leg bent at the knee behind him," she said. "The poor guy just couldn't get his leg out! His face was dirty and tearstained; he was hungry, thirsty, and half-eaten by mosquitoes. When the police finally dug his leg out of the hole, he claimed he'd seen a talking dog doing the backstroke!" She was laughing at this point, and we all joined in.

"I hope he learned a lesson from all this," I said. "A talking dog, huh? Poor Beulah."

It was nice to be home and know that real life had kept on going and oh so nice to sleep in our own beds that night.

We had enjoyed a couple of days of lying around, not really doing anything other than going over the information the kids were given the last day of the Three Fires club. We knew it was in this information that we would find the most help, but what was it? There was something that we just kept missing. We almost knew it by heart. It was always on our minds; we dreamed about it, talked about it, and read it again. I wondered if we were going to figure this out before school started back up. It was already the end of August, and just like the summer had hit us hot and hard, fall seemed to come overnight.

Laura Jones' first letter brought quite a bit of excitement to the kids; it was addressed to all three of them, so Apples appointed herself the official reader.

Dear fellow Anishinabeks,

Sorry I could not write earlier, but my dad made me go to a camp for the kids of firefighters. Except for sliding down the pole, I was BORED! BORED! BORED!

That is, unless I was thinking of you all, which I did every day, so that helped.

What I really would like to know, though, is what you learned in the Three Fires club after I left. Can you write the information down and send it to me?

Were you able to get a medicine bag for me yet? I can't wait!

Your friend forever, Laura!

"I will write the letter, Charlie, and you read me the information as I write," said Christopher, who had pen and paper ready.

"What should I do?" Emma wanted to know.

"You go get an envelope and a stamp, then make sure Charlie doesn't accidentally leave anything out," Christopher said.

"Christopher, you seem to be in a hurry about this," I said, laughing. I had never seen him in such a hurry in his life!

"Mom, school starts in a week," he replied. "If I don't do it now, I may not have time later." That is what he said, but I could tell he really liked Laura.

"Well, Ah think Ah should be the one that reads the information to you," Apples said. "Ah have feelings, you know, and you have hurt them again." Apples dabbed at her eyes with the back of her paw as she said this.

Such a drama queen, I thought.

"OK, OK, you read the information, and I will think as you read," said Charlie, who was already deep in thought.

So, for the hundredth time, the information was read. This time, though, it was read slowly so that Christopher could write it down.

"When a Native American died," Apples read aloud, "the body was placed on a platform."

Christopher repeated each word as he wrote: "—placed on a platform."

"Their feet pointed to the west," Apples continued.

"Their feet pointed to the west," they all repeated.

"They would be left for four days to allow their spirit to leave their body," Apples read.

Emma stopped repeating at that point to say, "Poor Wanderer! He was never found, so maybe his spirit couldn't leave his body."

At that instant, Apples' blue eye twitched, but I was the only one who noticed it.

"Well, of course Ah noticed it, too! Do you want the readers to think Ah ahm stupid or something?"

"Apples, I meant that besides you, I was the only one who noticed it. One would assume that if one's eye was twitching that one would be very aware of it!"

"Ah just want the readers to be informed that Ah did notice it, too."

Anyway, Apples' eye twitched, and the kids began to consider that since Wanderer's body was never found, he had to be left outside long enough for his spirit to leave it.

Apples read the next part: "After the four days, the body would then be wrapped in birch bark. If they were warriors, the body would be placed in a sitting position. If not, the body would be placed in a reclining position."

"Wanderer would be in a reclining position, then, wouldn't he?" Charlie asked.

"What does 'reclining' mean, anyway?" Emma wanted to know.

"It means leaning back in a relaxed position. What else does it say?" asked Christopher, who was anxious to move on.

Apples read further, "The medicine man then put a hole in each item belonging to the dead, and they were buried with the body."

As Christopher was writing this down, Charlie asked, "Why did they put a hole in the items? I forgot what Little Bear said about it." He had been lying on his stomach but sat up as he said this.

"Remember, he said it was so that the spirit of the item would be released from it—so that it could go on the journey with the person and be useful in the next life," Christopher reminded him.

"Yah, that's what it says here, too," Apples added as she looked at the notes.

"Oh yeah, write that down, too; it might be important," said Charlie, who was back on his stomach, head held in hands, thinking.

Emma was lying on the chair with her feet up on the wall behind her. Her dark ponytail feathered out on the floor. Christopher sat cross-legged with the book he was using as a writing table on his lap, chewing on the pen.

They were all busy thinking. It had become so quiet that I could hear the hall clock tick, a sound not heard very often in our house.

They sat in silence like that for quite some time, then Christopher got up, went to his room, and came back with the snow snake.

"What does the rest of it say?" he asked.

Apples had to be woken up to continue: "After the burial, a totem was placed upside down, and a fire would be burned another four days to light the way to the path of souls."

"—the path of souls," Christopher said as he finished writing.

Charlie, who now had the snow snake, asked, "Where is the hole?"

With eyes wide and round, all three of them asked, "Yeah! Where is the hole?"

For the first time in a long time, we all felt like we might actually be getting somewhere. The finished letter was sent to Laura.

Writing the information down step-by-step very slowly had given them time to consider that the snow snake had never been properly readied for burial.

The kids wasted no time in planning a quick trip back to the grave to see if Wanderer's other belongings that lay there in the earth were properly readied for burial.

Wednesday morning we were off on our mission, hoping it just looked like a normal walk. Christopher, deep in thought, had the dog's leash, Charlie had on his usual sideways hat, and Emma was humming a tune. We turned into the cemetery, walked our usual path, and not one of us knew he was there. None of us, including Apples, saw him. He must have been sneaking around not wanting us to notice him. Or we were just too intent on the day's mission to notice him.

Apples held out her ears, one for Charlie and one for Christopher. I held Christopher's hand, and Emma had Charlie's.

"Think about Wanderer's belongings," I said.

"EDD..............IEEEE!!!" Emma's yell ripped through time!

Eddie had grabbed Emma's free hand!

"Oh, Eddie, oh Eddie!" I gasped.

"Why are you always sneaking around, Eddie?" Christopher said. "You need to stop playing these ridiculous games!" Christopher had let go of Apples' leash and had his hands on Eddie's shoulders, and Charlie quickly put the boy into a headlock.

Eddie was shaking and sputtering, "I'm sorry! So, so sorry. Why am I such a kook? I'm sorry."

"Oh, PAA-LEESE let meh slap him with mah tail! Just one mighty, teach-him-a-lesson slap! PAAA-LEE-EE-EE-ES!!" I guess I don't have to tell you that it was Apples talking.

When Charlie let him go, Eddie asked, "Whe... whe... where am us, I mean I?" His black curls hung around his round face, making him look like an innocent cherub.

"Listen, Eddie, we are not going to tell you where we are, and we are not going to tell you how we got here, and we are not going to tell you what we are doing here, and you are *never* going to tell *anyone*, anywhere, *ever* about this—or I will tell everyone that *you* were the one who took the donation money and buried it in the dunes!" Christopher said all of this much more calmly than his reddened face appeared.

"How did you—? Who told you—? I WON'T, I WON'T! BUT— BUT— But your dog *CAN* ta— *talk*!!" Eddie sputtered.

"Yah, about that," said Emma, doing her best Apples impersonation. "Ah ahm the Queen of Dog World, and Ah...."

I interrupted her with: "Oh!! For Pete's sake! Everyone just calm down!"

Apples moved behind Eddie and gave her "pocket" a lick. She took out her medicine bag and shook it well. She bellowed out quite the howl, and just like that, Eddie fell asleep. I couldn't breathe normally for a minute, and Apples told us to move Eddie to the twin angels statue.

"Sheesh, Apples, I didn't even know you *had* a medicine bag," Charlie said.

"Yah, that's because it was in mah pocket," Apples replied. "There is a lot of cool stuff Ah collected in mah travels in mah pocket! WAAA-waa-HAA!"

"Well, how did you know you could put Eddie to sleep?" Christopher wanted to know.

"Ah guess Ah saw it somewhere—maybe," she said.

"Is he going to be OK?" Emma asked with a furrowed brow.

"Yah, he will think he was dreaming, Ah hope," Apples said.

"Good Lord, I hope so, too! We need to hurry and get home," I said. "This is the most ridiculous day of my life!"

Poor Eddie, poor, poor, boy! I would have to think of a way to make this up to him someday—maybe by writing a book about this someday and dedicating it to him.

The grave was open and exposed, and we could see that every single item was like new. Not even one had a hole drilled in it. Why? What did that mean? Could this be the key to unlock that door of mystery that had stood before us all summer?

Yes, we were making progress, and we would go back one more time. The Saturday before school started was the only day that Chet could join us. Saturday was just a few days away.

CHAPTER ELEVEN

SUMMER'S END

"I wish we didn't have to say goodbye to them," Emma said as we went over our plan again.

"None of us wants to say goodbye, but we can always cherish the time and the experiences we have had this summer," said Chet in an attempt to comfort her, but we all knew that saying goodbye would be the hardest part.

"Ah think you all should trust meh more than that," Apples interjected with her blue eye giving a wink. That is all she would say about it, which was kind of nice, if you know what I mean.

"Ah hope that you are not going to leave that silly remark in your book. It ruins the whole story. By now all the readers know how stupendous Ah ahm. They probably want to hear much more from meh and less from you. You know, Ah might just write mah own version of this story as it is. You just do not do meh justice."

"Yes, Apples, I am sure the public is amazed by you. Almost as sure as I am that they think you interrupt the story too much. I am also very sure that they want to know what happened, so if you will go lie down somewhere.... Not on the furniture!"

Jeans and sweatshirts were the attire for the day as we walked toward the cemetery. Fall was in the wind, and some leaves had already changed slightly, but summer was still standing her ground.

When we arrived at the twin angels, we had already decided what we were going to think about, so there was no discussion about it that time.

Before Chet and I each rubbed Apples' ear, we checked to make sure there would be no hitchhikers that day, then said aloud together, "Take us to Wanderer's village to end the sorrow of his people."

Something different than before happened. It was no longer the same time of year—it was much later in the fall. The leaves were rich in color. Deep reds, oranges, and golds painted parts of the blue sky, and as always, we were amazed.

We were invited to the fireside immediately and given blankets to warm ourselves with. It was as if some kind of holiday had been planned. Most of the Odawa were dressed in festive clothing. Moon-Deer and Standing-Elk were dressed very plainly compared to the others. When Charlie asked about it, Apples explained to us the Feast of the Dead.

"Each autumn a banquet is served, and a place is set for each person who has died in that year," Apples said. "This shows that the Odawa have not forgotten them and that their spirit lives with the Odawa. They remember Wanderer every year because he has not found his way to the path of souls. Those in plain dress represent the families of the dead."

With Apples interpreting, Chet said to the tribe, "We feel very honored to be here and accepted by all of you. We believe we have come with good news."

Standing-Elk stood to his feet, saying, "The spirits said you would come. We will hear the good news after we have the feast." With a wave of his hand, the whole community began preparations for the feast. Eventually we, too, became involved in the work. Christopher, Charlie, and the other boys began to bring water to the women cooking. Emma helped them prepare vegetables. Chet and Running Bear were in charge of the fish and game that many men had brought. All had a job to do, and all performed their duties cheerfully. Baskets, bowls, and clay jars were set out full of rice, berries, and the corn, beans, and squash we saw growing on a previous trip.

As we ate, we listened to the stories of loved ones who had passed on.

When Standing-Elk spoke of Wanderer, we listened carefully. He had taken off his beaded wampum belt and held it in his hands as he told his story. "Wanderer always said that he had a special purpose, that the Great Spirit often told him he would go on a profound journey with the wind—and that the journey would take him far—"

"—for this is your gift and ability," said Christopher, finishing this sentence with Standing-Elk.

Now all eyes were on him.

For the first time since we arrived, I looked at him, then at the rest of my family. Sitting there wrapped in woven blankets, we all looked as if we belonged there with them. I felt proud to be a part of them, and they were proud of us, too. I could tell by the way they looked at us. After the feast, the clothes of mourning were put away and their lives would return to more normal days.

"It is time for you to share the good news you have come with," Standing-Elk announced. We were promptly joined by the others who were eagerly waiting to hear what we had come to tell them.

Christopher told him about his dreams, how he was walking along the path of ice playing with the snow snake when a voice from the sky told him of a journey he would take. He said he believed Wanderer had drowned in the icy river. Charlie added that it probably happened when Wanderer was playing with the snow snake. They all nodded their heads as if to say they had figured the same thing. Chet told them about Mr. Bear and how he had been sent to us to help. Emma shared how Laura had helped by giving the dream catcher to Christopher. The Odawa appeared to be filled with pleasure as each part of the story unraveled.

Apples, who had never eaten better in her life than on that day, slept in between Standing-Elk and Moon-Deer as they each petted her. We had not said anything about what part she played in all of this; we knew we did not need to.

Christopher then explained how we had come to realize that the items left in Wanderer's grave had no holes drilled into them. The fire that moments before had burned bright was now dying down. All that was left was the soft glow of the coals. That seemed to set the mood for the whole tribe as they all sat deep in thought, very quiet with a peaceful glow of satisfaction.

We all sat with our thoughts until the coals no longer warmed us. The air was cool and the sky black but clear, and we could see stars for miles. The only sounds heard were the distant waves at the lake and the rustle of the wind in the leaves. The smell of autumn filled our lungs, and as the smoke from the fire faded and sleep was heavy upon us, Standing-Elk stood.

"Tomorrow, we leave for our winter home, and from there I will go to the grave of my son," he said. "Many of you have prayed to the Great Spirit, and now your prayers have been heard. Anyone who wishes is welcome to join me on this trip."

Immediately, all were standing. All—including the six of us.

CHAPTER TWELVE

JOURNEY

The next morning we awoke to find them all busy at work. We were given clothes to change into and moccasins to wear. We had been so tired the night before that we did not realize we had been sleeping in a wigwam! The excitement was hard for Chet and me to contain, let alone the kids. Everyone smiled and some even giggled when they saw us dressed like them, but they all continued with their work. We joined in quickly.

The wigwams were dismantled and loaded into canoes. Wild rice, dried fruits and vegetables, nuts, dried meats, and grains were packed and ready to take to their winter home. These were all covered by furs and blankets, making them look like huge bundles.

The elderly and sick rode in canoes, and the rest of us walked.

Before anyone would leave, Standing-Elk led them in a ceremony of thanksgiving. They sang songs to the earth, thanking her for giving them a place to stay and for the food she had given them.

The trees were thanked for the gift of shelter they had given all summer. The wild animals that had given themselves for food were also thanked, and promises were made that they would return the care they had received. It had been a very good year; the Great Spirit had given them favor with the earth. They were full from her gifts. Offerings of seeds and tobacco were left to show their gratitude.

I could tell the sky would stay gray all day. The clouds that had formed were various shades of gray and looked angry, but this did not hinder the beauty of the forest at all. The leaves were at their peak in color, and when the wind blew, the leaves slapped at the sky as if to say, *It is not time for winter yet. Stay away for now.*

Christopher, Charlie, and Emma walked ahead with the children. It was hard to pick them out of the group because they were dressed in the deerskins and leggings that the Odawa wore. We could hear the soft songs they sang as they walked. The songs were about how the squirrels, foxes, beavers, badgers, deer, rabbits, and other animals would spend their winter. They sang of the brave birds that would stay through winter and those that would leave and bring spring back with them.

Apples was running alongside us the whole way with the many dogs that loved the Odawa. I thought it was funny that she had not spoken one word, unless she had to quickly translate a thing or two, since we arrived here this time. She ran from person to person, licking their hands or chasing an occasional stick one of the children threw. One thing I had to admit was that the other dogs really did act like she was their queen. They let her choose first from the food they caught and gave her the nicest place to sleep. Christopher and Charlie noticed it, too. I could see the pride in their faces whenever they petted the self-proclaimed Queen of Dog World.

We had walked all day. We did not even stop for lunch; dried meats and fruit were eaten as we walked. The earthy smell of fall seemed to surround us in hope and energy, exciting us all for the trip.

Nonetheless, we were very glad to stop and rest when evening came.

Small fires were built and stories told as we ate supper. Since we were not used to so much walking, we were all exhausted. Two of the Native American men showed us how to make beds in the leaves by rolling up into a blanket and burying ourselves in the leaves. This would keep us warm and protect us from wind and some rain if need be.

We were alone as a family for the first time that day.

"I know why we have to go to the winter home first," said Christopher from one of the leaf piles. "We have to go to the place that Wanderer died to try to capture his spirit."

"I bet you are right! I have been thinking about that all day myself," Chet said from his own pile of leaves.

"Well, I knew there must be a good reason for it because of the way everyone so readily accepted it. So, here I am trying to sleep in a leaf bed," I mumbled, half asleep.

Emma's was the last voice I heard: "I love the way my leaf bed smells. I am going to put leaves in my bed from now on."

We woke up to the smell of rain; it was drizzling. We ate some corn cakes with some kind of berry sauce on them. Charlie loved them; I think he ate six of them. Chet and I really wanted a cup of coffee to wake us up and warm our bones. Moon-Deer and Standing-Elk didn't seem to mind the discomforts, nor did the others.

The meal did not take long, and then everybody was ready to go. Bundles were set on backs and on canoes. Day two had begun.

Luckily, it did not drizzle long. The sun came out, and it was a beautiful day.

The river we were following had widened and the trees were farther apart, which allowed plenty of sunshine through. The boys were busy spearing fish in this area, so we knew there would be fresh fish for supper.

Emma and the girls were running along collecting the last of the fall berries.

I loved how these people took advantage of every situation as it arose. We had come to a wonderfully scented grove of pines, and their soft needles covered the floor of the forest. Many ladies began to gather them for the floors of their wigwams. The larger needles were also collected to use as sewing needles. Baskets were filled with stones, feathers, and pretty leaves to use as decoration on clothing. Many plants were added to use as dyes and for medicines.

We gathered, sang, laughed, played—and walked and walked and walked!

We stopped a little earlier than we had the day before. We had made good progress, and we had the wonderful fish to prepare for supper. So, that fish and roasted corn made our supper.

We sat around a big fire that night while the dancers danced and sang. Games, including something like leapfrog, were played by people of all ages, and of course there were prayers.

The moon was full and luminous. It lit up the night and gave us a sense of well-being. Our leaf beds were very comfortable as we drifted off to the most pleasant dreams we had ever had.

"I wish I did not have to wake up," Charlie said sleepily, rolling over in the leaves. "I dreamed I was a bear and had all the berries and corn cakes that I would ever want in my cave. I was totally ready to hibernate all winter."

"That is kind of the way my dream went, too, but I was a bunny with a marvelous fur bed deep in my burrow," said Emma, hugging her knees to herself as if she was still snuggling in that fur.

"I dreamed I was a deer and had found a splendid home for the winter for my fawns," I said. "An old tree had fallen, its branches had formed a sheltered area, and the ground below was grassy and soft." I smiled as I remembered my dream and tried to get the leaves out of Emma's hair.

Chet shared his dream next. "My dream was very similar to all of yours, only I was a fox, I had a home in the side of a hill in the roots of a tree, and my bed was made out of leaves, of all things!" he said, laughing. Then he asked, "What was your dream, Christopher?"

"l dreamed that I was Wanderer, but this time I was safe in the arms of my people," Christopher said.

As we walked that day, a man named Bear-Claw explained that we had met our animal guides in our dreams and that we could now look to them in times of trouble and they would help us. He then gave us new names. I became Sheltered-Fawn, and Chet was Fox-Heart. Emma's new name was Sleeping-Bunny, and Charlie loved his new name: It was Bear-with-a-Full-Tummy. Christopher, of course, was given Wanderer's name of Wind-Traveler.

On day three, the wind picked up and brought with it very cold air. Fur blankets were removed from the canoes, and we were each given one. This helped keep the wind and the cold out, but this could not be September. It became colder and colder. The leaves that had been so beautiful just the day before were no longer in the trees. Time was speeding up somehow. It seemed as though Chet and I were the only ones who noticed.

"It acts like the end of November out here! What in the world is going on?" Chet asked Apples.

Apples was not sure what was happening, and I could tell it bugged her, because her brown eye rolled just a bit when she answered. Winter was in the sky, and the message was clear: Snow before morning!

Standing-Elk said that we were almost to the winter grounds, but it seemed like the winter grounds were coming to us.

By noon on the third day, we arrived at the winter home. This area was selected because of the excellent hunting and thick trees that provided extra shelter from wind and winter storms.

If they had planned on staying for the winter, they would have put up the wigwams, but because we were there for a very different reason, small shelters were put up and fires were built instead to protect us from the now icy wind.

Christopher recognized this area from his dreams. "This is the river Wanderer was playing by!" he said. "It was farther downstream that he disappeared, though."

Other boys agreed that it was farther down that they had last seen him.

"We will go to the spot where he last had life tomorrow," said Standing-Elk. "The ceremony will be performed there, and we will ask the spirits to hear us one more time." Standing-Elk was then joined by others in song as he prayed to the Great Spirit. He and several others began a fast that would last until they beheld Wanderer.

The snow that the clouds had promised us had begun. The wind had died down so that the snow fell softly.

We had all transformed into Native Americans as best as could be expected. The kids were equipped with the same gear the other children had. The boys had tried their hand at hunting and spearing fish with the bows and spears they had been given. At night they had made arrows for themselves by firelight.

Emma's friends had braided her hair with shells and feathers in it.

I felt like we were becoming one with nature, and we learned respect for our earth. I knew none of us would ever forget this.

"Mom, do you think school has started yet?" Emma asked. "I mean, we have been here a very long time. What if we can't go home?" Her eyes were wide with the question, but she did not seem worried at all.

"We will have to go back—we will never really belong here," Christopher replied. "We do not understand their ways and religions. It is what people believe that separates them from others." Christopher, at age twelve, had figured out something that other people never do.

"Did you figure this out on your own, or did someone just tell you this?" Chet asked in amazement.

"I guess I just know," Christopher said. "I know that people came to this country for religious freedom and then tried to change the religions of the people who already lived here. Now that I know the Odawa, I don't see anything wrong with the way they believe, and I believe that Jesus will find them and loves them, too." Christopher squinted and nodded as he spoke.

My son, at twelve, was much wiser than many grown people.

"Well, why couldn't we just learn to believe the way they do, then, but add Jesus?" Emma asked again.

"Adding Jesus, really, is the most important part," I said, giving her a hug.

"Maybe we could, but that is not the reason we came here," Christopher was saying.

Then Charlie interrupted, "For real! I, for one, also believe in TV, Nintendo, movies, skateboards—and I would love a Pop-Tart about now."

"That explains everything," Chet said, laughing.

"I have to admit that I do miss my own bed and bathroom, too, but Christopher is right," I said. "We came here for a reason. I almost think I could get used to this, though."

"And when we are done, we must leave," Christopher said with finality. "I just don't think we should take the chance of changing them in any way. We are the ones who will be changed, and then we will go home." It seemed like Wanderer himself would have said this if he could have.

CHAPTER THIRTEEN

PROMISE KEPT

Moon-Deer and Standing-Elk were clothed in ceremonial dress when we walked the short distance to where Wanderer had last been seen.

Tobacco burned in several pots along the river as songs were offered up in prayer. A larger ornamental pot was placed at Standing-Elk's feet. He said nothing as he held his ceremonial stick, decorated with feathers and beads, out over the water.

The wind blew across his fur coat, ruffling it. The snow that was still falling glistened in the sun's light. Standing-Elk's headdress, too, was blowing in the wind. Its black and white feathers seemed to have life as they flew in all directions, yet the headdress stayed tight to his head.

The songs grew louder for a while, then subsided to a quiet hum. Many tears were shed.

Still, Standing-Elk did not say a word, but remained with arms outstretched. Moon-Deer stood beside him and shed many tears, yet she, too, stood quiet and motionless. Small pinecones, porcupine quills, and strips of dyed leather decorated her skirt and sleeves. Her hair blew free in the wind around her. Their bare hands were red in the cold.

The sweet smell of tobacco burned on and on. I was not sure if it was the smell of tobacco, the freezing cold, or the fact that Moon-Deer had been fasting since the Feast of the Dead, but she fell forward onto the ground and stayed there until the tobacco burned out.

Christopher was asked to lower a wooden container into the water to take some up. He then mixed ashes from the ornamental pot into the water. Standing-Elk put a lid onto it, and with that, the ritual was finished.

The water represented Wanderer's spirit, and the ashes represented that the Great Spirit, giver of all life, was with them.

A small thanksgiving ceremony was performed. Fish and seeds were buried along the riverbed to thank her for her part in all this.

Travel had become more difficult without the use of snowshoes. One man named Brave-Wolf helped Chet make us each a pair by taking small twigs and soaking them until they could be easily shaped. Then they used spruce roots and wove them around the frame.

We would not have to wear these for very long, though. We found that, as we traveled to where Wanderer's grave had been, winter was reversing itself.

Snow stopped falling, leaves returned to the trees in full autumn colors, and the air grew warmer. The fur blankets and snowshoes were returned to the canoes.

Wanderer had died in the winter, but his grave was not prepared for him until the following fall.

We could see the Great Spirit was at work.

Soon Wanderer would walk the path of souls like those before him.

That night, as we ate pheasant and squirrel with wild rice, we talked about how little of what had happened had been explained to us. They just assumed that we knew what and why they were doing all this. We liked feeling that, on some level, we did.

The mood around the main fire that night was quieter than usual. There was a sacredness about it, with great assurance that a promise was soon to come. The black eyes of the people flickered back the reflection of the fire and were full of hope and adventure. Even their dogs appeared to be full of anticipation.

"I wonder what will happen, exactly?" Charlie said.

"I am not sure, but I have a feeling that, come this time tomorrow, we will know," Chet answered.

We knew this trail was very near Wanderer's grave. These were the dunes that we, too, called home. We had been walking toward Lake Michigan over the past two days, and it was a comfort to hear the waves off in the distance and realize how close to home we really were.

In the early afternoon the next day, we all gathered around the gravesite, and again many people began to sing and pray. Tobacco was burned. A great torch was lit and placed at the head of the grave near the tribal totem that had been placed and was waiting for this time. The kids remembered much of what Little Bear had taught them as they watched this ritual unfold. Normally the torch would have burned for four days while the spirit left the body of the deceased, but since Wanderer's spirit had become one with the river, the four-day wait was not necessary.

The rectangular log structure that had become the final resting place for Wanderer's belongings was now being opened. The bowl containing the water and ashes was placed at the foot of the grave, and pots of burned tobacco ashes were poured out around the grave. Then fresh tobacco was placed in the grave where the items belonging to Wanderer had been.

Standing-Elk and Moon-Deer knelt at each side of the grave. They had been fasting since the Feast of the Dead and could barely stand, but they could pray.

Each item from the grave was chanted over individually by Standing-Elk. These items were then given to a man who drilled a hole in each one with what looked like a tool made especially for that use.

First, a necklace made from claws of a bear, then an arrow, a small drum, a beautifully decorated shirt, and, of course, the snow snake. These, along with the bowl of water and ash, were put into the grave now filled with burning tobacco.

Voices rose in chants. Thick tobacco smoke filled the air and our lungs.

Apples, who now wore a feathered headdress, continued explaining anything we did not understand.

Drums beat, and rattles shook. The chanting grew wilder and sounded like the yips and caws of animals in danger. Several men danced a wild spinning dance, and women groaned, cried, and occasionally let out high-pitched wails.

Even though I hate to admit it, I think we were all scared half to death.

"This is why we came, isn't it?" Chet asked. "We cannot chicken out on them now. This is their way. Remember, we do not have to understand it, but we will respect it."

"I am not afraid," said Christopher, who was really the only one of us who could honestly say that. He didn't appear to be afraid at all. Poor Emma was crying with her face in her hands, and Charlie, who had turned gray with fear, was swinging his medicine bag over his head and yelling as loud or louder than the rest of them.

The wild dancing and chanting were swirling together and working into a fury.

Standing-Elk and Moon-Deer seemed to be in a trance, while others seemed near delirium. The smoke had become so thick that it was hard to tell if it was daytime or nighttime.

Then, it happened: Wanderer stood in the center of what would have been his grave. Slightly darker in appearance than Christopher, they could have been twins, their faces identical with the same nose, eyes, and smiles.

As the tobacco burned out, Christopher and Wanderer stood face-to-face in the grave, clasping hands to wrists—a gesture of true friendship.

Wanderer then knelt next to each of his parents and spoke to them, thanking them for bringing him into this world, not once, but twice.

Although they were both exhausted from the ritual, they shed tears of joy that their son had returned from the journey that the Great Spirit had sent him on.

All sorrow was soon forgotten and replaced with much rejoicing.

Even the dogs jumped about, tails wagging and barks ringing.

Many of the people began to build fires, and food was brought out and prepared. That night would be a great celebration.

Wanderer had returned.

The weather was perfect for a party. The air was crisp and fresh, and the sky wore its brightest cornflower blue. Of course, the trees wore their most brightly colored leaves, displaying reds, golds, oranges, and yellows, all dressed up for the occasion.

After much eating, the Odawa changed into their festive dress.

The deerskin cloth had been decorated with feathers of many different colors. Dyed seeds were sewn onto clothes in beautiful designs. Woven grasses and dyed porcupine quills were also used in hair and on instruments. Headdresses, bustles, and jewelry were worn by many.

As we all sat in a large circle around the dancers, we all sang and chanted. A smaller circle of musicians played drums of different shapes and sizes, shook rattles, and played flutes made of reeds and wood. Perfect rhythm was kept by all in song, music, and dance.

Smiling children with hands on hips and tilted heads danced, and their feet moved in unison. The adults watched with pride and approval at their young ones.

When the young ladies danced, they wore the robes they had crafted, showing their many talents. Long black braids with dyed grasses trailed down their sides or backs as they moved together in a circle. The ankle bracelets they wore kept time with the drumbeat, adding depth to the sights and sounds of the celebration.

The young men's dance was much livelier. Some had painted faces, and long headdresses of feathers flowed down their backs. Their bustles of every color made them look like huge, beautiful birds. They danced by, bending low, turning around, jumping, or hopping on one foot.

The colors swirled as the excitement rose.

When Wanderer joined them in his form from three hundred years before, the atmosphere was changed to new levels of passion, and he taught Christopher and Charlie a dance.

Hoots and howls rose from the onlookers as the young men danced. That time we all hooted and howled, not in fear, but in happiness for a job well done.

The dancing continued for hours, sometimes involving old men and sometimes young children. Everyone joined in at several points.

What an amazing honor it was to have been included in the turning, twirling dances under the stars with the full moon brightly lighting the show.

We found our way to leafy beds and fell asleep that night totally exhausted. It had been a full day, to say the least. As we drifted off to sleep, the drums continued to beat, and many dancers continued to celebrate the mystical return of one who was lost so very long ago.

CHAPTER FOURTEEN

PATH OF SOULS

"Mom, Dad, wake up! Come on, wake up!" said Christopher and Charlie as they urgently shook us awake. "Listen, it has stopped! The drums have stopped."

"The quiet seems strange. What is wrong?" Charlie asked.

I tried to sound reassuring as I said, "I am sure everyone has gone to sleep; it is very late."

Apples just returned from somewhere in the brush. Her blue eye was winking. She said, "Ah think you are about to have the experience of your lives. Come on, follow meh. You don't have to rub mah ears for this one."

The moon was still very full and bright. The stars seemed so close that if we had stood on tiptoes, it seems we could have touched them.

Apples had led us out of the dunes to the shores of the lake where the moon's reflection across the water added to the supernatural mood of the evening. Like magic, it had caused the sky and water to become one.

We watched as the Odawa were leaving. They walked out upon the water and into the sky; the Milky Way was there to greet them. As they continued farther into the sky, they were transformed into spirit beings. Some walked, some flew, and some paddled canoes, and most of them became the spirits of animals.

It was then that we realized what was meant by "the path of souls."

"I guess this is the end of our mission," Chet said to Standing-Elk, stretching out his hand in a gesture of respect and farewell.

Standing-Elk gave Chet a gentle nod and said, "I hope not, for there is still much for you to do."

"We believe that you must remember what you have learned and encourage the Anishinabek not to forget their great heritage," said Moon-Deer, whose eyes were as round and bright as the full moon above.

Wanderer's smile shone in the night as he explained, "I have traveled a great distance to find you, to bring you here to learn from your people. I understand what the Great Spirit meant when He spoke of the journey that would take me far. I have traveled to a time I did not know, to a place that had been my home but is my home no more. I have found you, and you have released my spirit from travel. It is given now to you to tell the story to our people. Our people should remember our heritage, for it is good and true."

There were only a few Odawa left on the shore, but we watched as the rest of them filled the night as bears, wolves, bobcats, foxes, deer, squirrels, rabbits, chipmunks, buffalo, and elk.

I felt my heart breaking as we held them close and promised to encourage Native Americans to keep their heritage and to be proud of it.

The children's closest friends had stayed as long as possible. Goodbyes were said, and promises never to forget one another were made.

"We are proud to call you friends and honored to call you ancestors," Chet said as he kissed Moon-Deer on the cheek and gave a bear hug to Standing-Elk.

I just wept. I cannot talk and cry at the same time.

Christopher and Wanderer had clasped hands to wrists. "In your dreams, brother," Wanderer said with a tear in his eye.

"In your heart," Christopher replied, his voice catching with emotion.

After thanking the queen of Dog World for being such a good interpreter throughout the whole adventure, Wanderer then gave Christopher a medicine bag and said, "Give this to Laura for me! She is cute!"

"Hey, wait a minute—how do you know about her?" Christopher asked in amazement.

Wanderer laughed and replied, "I've been everywhere, like the wind, for a long time."

Wanderer just smiled and turned to go, then stopped and said, "Go ahead and tell Mr. Bear about all this. He will believe you; his dog talks, too. Oh, and be a good *wiijkewenmaa,* a good friend, to Eddie—he will need one."

The three of them were the last ones left. As they walked out onto the water and into the sky, Moon-Deer became a beautiful doe, translucent and shining like the full moon. Standing-Elk stopped and stood looking at us for what seemed like a long time, the night stars shining around him. Then he finally turned and walked out onto the moon's reflection on the water. As he was transformed in spirit into an elk, he sped off into the night sky and into the Milky Way as strong and majestic as he was in human form.

Wanderer smiled and sang as he left: "Thank you, thank you! I knew you would figure it out." Then he swirled around and around—and became the wind. He was no longer seen but would be forever felt.

We awoke Sunday morning in our own beds, in our own clothes, the same beds and clothes we had had for years—but we were not the same, and we never would be again.

The snow snake was no longer under Christopher's pillow. In its place was the wampum belt that Standing-Elk had worn. The story the wampum belt told was of a lost boy who would someday be found through the help of children of the New World and their dog.

"They knew all along," Chet stated.

"Well, of course we did!" Apples said. "Ah say we, because Ah knew the whole time. Ah just thought it would be a great summer if Ah kept you all guessing, and that is exactly what Ah did, too. You didn't have one eensy-beensy clue the whole time! Ah thought Ah was going to crack up when Ah saw how scared you all were when they were burning tobacco and chanting. Ah mean, what do you expect when the Queen of Dog World lives at your house, anyway?"

That night we took Apples to the ice cream parlor and let her have as much ice cream as she wanted. Between the brain freeze and the sick tummy, she had to be carried home over Chet's shoulder with her tongue hanging out, but she was happy!

"Now we can tell them about the time...."

"Apples, that will have to be another story."

"Yah, Ah know they want to know why Eddie was sitting on our front porch with a suitcase when we got home."

THE END

EPILOGUE

You might think that one such an adventure like this one would have been enough for any family.

I certainly do, but what about Eddie? Did he really think he had just dreamed about his hijacking a time travel?

He knew Apples could talk and that the Heron family was well, different.

There is so much more he wants to find out.

Tails of Time Travel Two just may have the answers.

ABOUT THE AUTHOR

 Winnie Garza is a retired life enrichment coordinator with a Certified Dementia Practitioner (CDP) certification. The time spent with her seniors will always hold a special place in her heart. She raised her two sons along the shores of Lake Michigan, in west Michigan, where she now resides with her husband of fifty years. They enjoy biking, camping, boating, spending time at the beach, and going on outings with friends. Her greatest joy is time spent with family, which includes a grandson and a granddaughter, and yearly vacations spent together. Winnie also enjoys hiking, gardening, embroidery, decorating, and cooking. She loves words and how, when used with wisdom, they are helpful and healing, and when woven together, they tell a great story.

www.ingramcontent.com/pod-product-compliance
Lightning Source LLC
Chambersburg PA
CBHW071305130626
46556CB00004B/1478